northward to the moon

northward to the moon

polly horvath

Groundwood Books / House of Anansi Press
Toronto

Groundwood Books / House of Anansi Press
110 Spadina Avenue, Suite 801, Toronto, Ontario M5V 2K4

We acknowledge for their financial support of our publishing program the
Canada Council for the Arts, the Government of Canada through the Canada
Book Fund (CBF) and the Ontario Arts Council.

 Canada Council   Conseil des Arts   ONTARIO ARTS COUNCIL
for the Arts   du Canada   CONSEIL DES ARTS DE L'ONTARIO

Library and Archives Canada Cataloguing in Publication
Horvath, Polly
Northward to the moon / Polly Horvath.
ISBN 978-0-88899-999-3
I. Title.
PS8565.O747N67 2010   jC813'.54   C2010-900102-8

Design by Rachael Cole
Cover illustration by Matt Mahurin

Printed and bound in Canada

To Arnie, Em and Becca

contents

We Become Outlaws

Our family lasted almost one year in Saskatchewan. It took the town that long to figure out that Ned didn't speak any French.

"I always looked on it as kind of a frill," he explains to my mother.

"French?"

"Teaching," says Ned. "I coach the girls' basketball team and keep real good order in the classroom, so the kids don't, you know, go out and smoke in the hallways, at least during class time, and I always help out at assemblies. I was the one who rustled up some World War Two veterans for Remembrance Day. Remember, Jane, the knack I had with the veterans?"

"Knack with the veterans?" asks my mother. She seems stunned by recent events.

"You don't want them drooling on their shoes. And you want them to look like they're having fun even if they've forgotten what they're doing there. It takes a certain deft touch," says Ned.

"So you didn't think knowing French was really so important?" My mother is trying just desperately to understand Ned's point of view.

"Not in the general scheme of things," says Ned cheerfully.

"Well!" says my mother. "Are they *angry*?"

"Oh, livid," says Ned.

"I guess they want you to resign?" asks my mother.

My heart leaps up at the thought of leaving this crummy little house on the edge of town where we have lived for the last year. None of us have warmed to Saskatchewan. We moved here from Massachusetts the summer before when my mother married Ned, who got a full-time job here. His first full-time job ever. But it turns out that there is more to life than this.

The town has financed this house for us but at

great cost. There is no one very rich in town but still we are despised and pitied for the charity they afford us, giving us this house and lending us this furniture. I have no friends here. It is rumored we get our clothes off the dump. I don't mind so much for me but it is very hard on Maya, who has never had her own friends and wants some desperately. She has one so-called friend named Katie, who lords it over Maya and her poverty-stricken state. She is always saying things like she will give Maya her dolls when she outgrows them, knowing full well that by that time Maya will have outgrown them too.

We are not really so poverty-stricken. We have not had chicken and rice without the chicken once since moving. There is always food and heat. But whereas back in Massachusetts our house on the beach carried some cachet, it is different here. No one cares that my mother is a poet. Once at a school dessert night one of the moms asked me what my mother did for a living and when I said she was a poet the mom replied, "Don't worry, she'll get over that." I know that none of this bothers my mother but I am bothered on her account.

The only thing that has given us any respectability is Ned's position as the new French teacher.

"*Resign?* Are you kidding? They *fired* me. Darn shortsighted. You know I was one of only two male teachers in the whole frigging town," says Ned.

"Oh no!" says my mother. She looks so stricken that Ned and I glance at each other. But then the stricken feeling leaves her eyes and in its place I see the warm glow of possibilities. "But maybe," she goes on slowly, "this is a blessing in disguise. Now after the school year closes we can go back to Massachusetts. In the back of our minds, we always had that as a place to return."

I am not so sure that this was as true for Ned, and I snap my head back around to look for his response. His eyes are flickering, full of thought, but moving too quickly for me to detect anything definite. My mother's eyes are quiet, still waters running deep. My mother's deep waters all lead to us. I don't think any of us know where Ned's waters run. Or what his deep well holds behind those constantly flickering eyes. But between the two of them, from these mainspring places, the fate of me and my sister and brothers and our six destinies will be decided.

"Well, gosh darn it, gosh darn it all to heck! I didn't want to leave *this* way," he says at last. He has cleaned up his language considerably since marrying my mother and moving in with us and I mourn the loss. His salty language was expressive and lovely—poetry in its own way. "I was a role model for boys who want to teach. Now what are they to do?"

"They still have Mr. Christenson," I remind him.

"One male teacher means he is a blip in the natural order," says Ned, picking up an apple and chewing on it musingly. "Two says it's a respectable career choice."

I also pick up an apple and munch on it musingly, one leg tucked under me. I am thrilled at the idea of movement in any direction. I have been almost a year here and it has changed me.

The wide horizons of the prairies have caused me to pull in, to gather myself about and box myself carefully inside me, the way when you are outside and cold without a coat, you hug yourself to preserve your heat, to keep your vitality within. Maybe this accounts for the stoic unflinching faces of the prairie people. Maybe what I take for coldness or meanness is just the battening down of hatches against the inevitable blows from nature. And when they come, they come swiftly, unannounced and catastrophically. Crops gone in minutes from locusts. Sudden rains turning roads to flooding and unpassable mud. Lightning. Unchallenged unbarricaded winds. And there is not the rhythm of the ocean to keep you breathing. Instead perhaps you hunker down and hold yourself in against the deadly winters. The excitement but devastation of tornadoes. The look of the long lonely flat grasslands where you are exposed and vulnerable with nothing to hide behind. These people, dried and parched and suspicious and unwelcoming, may only be each holding on to themselves to keep from blowing away or withering in this place of capricious harm.

It has amazed me, as much as anything, that anyone would settle here forever and even try to keep such a town alive when letting it die might be best for all concerned. Then they could move to the seaside. Why would they spend a lifetime by choice in this dry place? It has been fascinating for comparative purposes. To see what people have and what they miss. To see what we have had and what we have not. But interesting is all it *has* been; it has never been an *us* place, it is a *them* place.

Maya hasn't been very happy but the boys, who are only six and four, fit in. They love the drifts and the cold. They love putting on their heavy snowsuits, pretending to be from space and building forts and rocket ships of snow. They love the dust storms and the lightning that flies across the prairies and the sudden thunderstorms and being sent home during tornado watches. The first time we heard prairie thunder rumbling far away on the horizon, Hershel said the sky was growling at us. It is a joy and wonder to him, a place where the sky takes note of us and speaks. Even in anger. He and Max are completely captivated by prairie dogs. They go out with their friends onto the grasslands to the prairie dog colonies and wait beside one of the many holes, guessing where the next prairie dog will emerge. I realize if they grow up here they will be prairie boys. This will be their place memory of growing up. It will separate us in a fundamental way. As if we will then belong to different places, they to the prairies and me to the

ocean. As if at some stage of our early development, our hearts take root in the landscape that
surrounds us and remain rooted there all our lives,
even when we're not.

I do not want them rooted somewhere different
from me. Families drift so easily anyway—look at
Ned's. He says probably nobody in his family even
knows where the other members are. Perhaps it is
an extreme case. I can't understand how someone
as nice as Ned could have lost track of his family
so easily and not seem to care. Could this happen
to me and Maya and Max and Hershel? I would
like us to make a pact saying it never will. I would
like to know that, even if it does, at least we are
united in the same memory of landscape.

"But didn't *you* learn French in school?" asks my
mother. How could Ned not know any French
when it is mandatory in Canada?

"Well, as you know, I didn't get much schooling.
At least in the early years. I managed to move
around often enough to avoid it."

Ned's mother had taken her eight children and
moved to Fort McMurray, Alberta, in the far north
after Ned's father took off one morning without a

word. Ned said his mother explained their father's speedy exit with "You never know what someone will up and do." As if an unpredictable universe were the one thing you could count on, and humans the most unpredictable element therein. Then she demonstrated it herself by moving them all from the civilized town of Edmonton to the wilds of Fort McMurray with seemingly nothing to offer in the way of employment for her or opportunities for them. In fact, it appeared that she had moved them for no reason at all. "She was true to her maxim," Ned said about his mother. "We could never tell what she was going to do."

Ned used to hitchhike to wherever he guessed his father was and visit him and then hitchhike back to see any brothers and sisters who were hanging around the house at the time. His mother hardly paid attention to anyone's comings and goings. They had been ripped out of a good Edmonton school and placed in a Fort McMurray school not so much bad as uninterested.

"Yep," said Ned when he related all this, "after my dad left she was pretty oblivious to the family in general. Mostly I came back when I ran out of money and needed a place to crash, although I generally preferred my father's when I could find him. On the other hand, Fort McMurray wasn't without *any* merit. You could go outside and see the northern lights any night in winter. Down south we had studied the northern lights but in Fort McMurray we experienced them. That's when I decided that experience is everything. That there was little I could learn in a classroom that was as worthwhile as seeing it for myself. So I hit the road and have been hitting it more or less ever since."

I am thinking about this conversation now. How Ned has managed to stay in one place with us for almost a year but how his feet must be itching for new experiences and that this business of being fired is a good excuse to go off and have more adventures. The problem is he has my mother to think of now and my mother clearly wants to go home.

I don't think putting down roots in Massachusetts is going to satisfy Ned and I am curious to see how he will resolve things but at that moment the phone rings. Ned picks it up. When he gets off, he says, "That was the oddest phone call. That was one of Mary's grandsons. Mary is dying."

"Who is that?" I ask.

"A friend from a long time ago," he says. "A long, long time ago." He stops and stares across the kitchen. He looks pale and strained.

"That woman who took you in all those years ago?" asks my mother.

"Yeah," says Ned.

"However did her grandson find you?"

"Through Canada 411. He's lucky. Any other year I wouldn't have had a fixed address or phone number."

"Why did Mary have to take you *in*? Why were you *out*?" I ask.

"I was lost. It's a long story. She must be about ninety now. He said she's really ill and drugged up and out of it but she keeps saying my name. They don't know why. They said that if I wanted to, I should come and see her because they don't think she has much time left."

"Of course you should!" says my mother.

"Yeah, but now I've got this whole firing thing hanging over my head," says Ned.

"Oh, Ned," says my mother. "What's done is done. This is more important, surely? Besides, now you don't have to take a leave of absence. You're *fired!*"

She makes it sound as if this has turned out to be fortuitously lucky.

"Let's all go!" says Ned, and he suddenly perks up. "Let's leave tonight under cover of dark!"

Finally, I think, an adventure. Ned had promised me nothing but adventures when we got to Canada but this is the first whiff I've caught of them.

"Leave like outlaws?" asks my mother.

I think she means it as a bad thing but she has chosen the wrong word for Ned. His eyes glow. "Like Jesse James!"

"Like Butch Cassidy and the Sundance Kid!" I say. I imagine us all on horseback with masks, robbing trains and making our way to Mexico. Ned gives me a wild look and I can tell we are having exactly the same fantasy. Life has been a little too mundane of late.

"But school!" says my mother.

For a poet she can be terribly prosaic sometimes.

"What school? You know what the last month of

school is like. There's nothing but cupcake days and field trips, right, Bibles?" Ned started calling me Bibles back in Massachusetts because I helped a mystical preacher deliver them for a while.

"Very true," I say.

"Besides," says Ned, "the children can hardly go back to the school that fired me. Think of the stigma. There's gonna be some stigma!"

"Oh, major stigma!" I say.

"The stigma," murmurs my mother, looking abstracted. This is all happening so fast. He was just fired this morning and already we're wearing masks and robbing trains.

"Let's leave tonight! Ned loves to drive at night," I say. We discovered this on the trip from Massachusetts to Saskatchewan. He says the roads are quieter and he likes to drive under the stars. "Let's take nothing but our clothes!"

————————

But in the coming days my mother insists on packing up the house properly and notifying banks and schools and the post office and other dull things.

Even Ned gives up his outlaw role and apologizes to the school for not knowing French.

"The board said they thought I was a darn good teacher anyway," Ned tells us later when he returns from school with his things. "And they didn't really care. Heck, they said they've known for years that Mrs. Cunningham doesn't know any math despite her degree. No, you know who wanted me fired? It's that lunatic fringe! That darn tiny group of parents who actually *care* what their children are learning. Let me tell you something, Jane, everyone is responsible for his own education. You can't teach anyone who doesn't want to learn and you can't stop a person who does."

This is such a stirring speech that we almost forget that the reason we are leaving is that in actual fact, you can't teach anyone something you yourself don't know.

"But you're still fired?" I ask hopefully.

I don't think Ned is paying attention to me. He is staring off into space ruminatively. "They should have hired me to teach Japanese. I *speak* Japanese."

"I didn't know you spoke Japanese," says my mother as she comes barreling through the room, her arms full of clothes to pack.

Ned breaks into a torrent of Japanese words.

"I'd love to learn Japanese. I always wanted to be better with languages," says my mother as she bustles up the stairs.

"I know a little Samoan too . . . ," Ned calls after her, and then he goes back to packing.

"Let's put bandanas on the lower parts of our faces as we drive out of town," I say to Ned, following him around and trying to recapture the spirit of our outlaw adventure through these never-ending closing-up chores.

"I think your mother is being flexible enough," says Ned, winking at me. "Letting us traipse here and there across Canada in a car. Let's just be costumed in our minds!"

"Sometimes I don't think you take this fully seriously," I say.

"*Au contraire, au contraire,*" says Ned, and then, whistling happily to himself, goes into the kitchen to help Max and Hershel, who are trying to pour themselves some milk and are about to spill it all over. "That's French, boys," he announces, jauntily opening the cookie jar.

"I told you he speaks French," says Max.

"I know," says Hershel solemnly.

They are like dogs, aware of so much and yet not, and at any rate, happy to follow the pack.

Maya is happy to leave because my mother says that after we drive to see Mary we are going back to Massachusetts. Sometimes I sense in Maya not just a desire but a real desperation to get home. I can never remember her being as cranky as she has become recently.

We all help my mother finish organizing and finally we find ourselves packed into our beat-up old station wagon, two adults, three children, me, my mother's box of books and a few suitcases.

We already live on the edge of town so in minutes we are beyond its tightly crossed legs and before us stretches the flat unforgiving land, the grass standing frozen and forlorn. There is nothing ahead but the horizon and the endless wintry road.

The Road

We stay in bad motels. Ned and I want to camp under the stars like Wild West outlaws but it is too cold. The Canadian winter is a blue icy vastness. Cold sends up waves from the earth just as heat does. You can see them like mirages over the highway. Sometimes it is so cold that you feel you could break off sheets of jagged frozen air, which would crunch like ice or glass, as deadly as any weapon. You don't want to fall through it. Every time we went outside this winter we gasped in disbelief; the cold like a vacuum sucks the warm breath out of you. It is hard to believe that anything can generate enough heat of its own to survive in this temperature. And yet bears roam and a

bit further north, caribou and wolves and arctic
fox and owl. The fires in their bellies enough to
keep them safe through the winter days. Now,
even in May, after the coldest winter on record, the
snow may be gone but the ground is still frozen.

We are three days on the road when I realize
that Ned hasn't told the story of his friend Mary
yet. He and my mother have obviously talked
about it but I have been so busy packing up that I
have forgotten to ask him.

"I don't see why we have to drive all the way
across the country just to see some old woman,"
says Maya to me. We are riding in the last row of
seats in the back of the station wagon, facing backward, as if we are perpetually waving goodbye.
"Why didn't we go home to Massachusetts and let
Ned go alone?"

"Because he probably wants Mama with him," I
say. "His friend is *dying*, Maya. She was important
to him at some point, I guess. Don't you want to
know why?"

"I don't care," says Maya. "I just want to go
home."

"Aren't you curious?"

"No. I want to read my comic book," says Maya maddeningly.

We don't speak for another half hour. Then as the car rolls down the road, with nothing of interest to see, and I fend off Maya, who has grown tired of her comic and is trying to give me a pedicure with no professional instruments or knowledge, I say, "Ned, where *exactly* are we going?"

Ned's face has the concentrated expression of someone going *to* somewhere. You can see him casting through his memories of this place from his past.

"To the Carriers," he says.

When my mother is at the wheel it makes her chatty but Ned drives silently most of the time. I think he goes to faraway places peacefully and contentedly in his head when he drives. I wonder if he is thinking about Mary dying or what has led him to this moment where he is in a car full of children heading to somewhere from his past. My mother lets him do this. She doesn't engage him in chitchat but instead, when she wants company, turns and talks to us in the back. Maya and I have to turn our heads around to talk to her.

"There's no place in Canada called Thecarriers," says Maya.

Maya since turning eight has become a great source of misinformation. She likes to expound on things she knows nothing about and when corrected isn't deterred in the least. At eight she is suddenly sure that she knows everything. I think we are all glad, if for nothing else on this adventure, that it has taken Maya away from her teacher, the cheerful, all-knowing Mrs. Gunderson. Mrs. Gunderson shared Maya's rarefied universe of misinformation. Seldom did a day go by when Maya didn't bring home some incredible statement of fact, some erroneous item of history, some word usage peculiar only to Mrs. Gunderson and Maya, which if you tried to correct it, brought a storm of tears and tantrums and the ultimate last word, "But Mrs. Gunderson *says* so." It was interesting if you thought of Maya and Mrs. Gunderson existing in their own little alternate universe. One in which its two citizens know everything. I listen to Maya ramble on about things she knows nothing about, more to find out what is happening in Mrs.Gunderson-land than to learn anything useful. I regard it as being like reading a good fantasy novel without having to go to the trouble of remembering endless ridiculous boring made-up names.

"I think the Carriers are a people, Maya," says my mother.

Now, as Ned doesn't further explicate, I ponder what carriers these are. I wonder if Ned, as he drives so dreamily down the long empty roads, has been inventing a Middle Earth–type fantasyland of his own, where people carry things. How would Mrs. Gunderson explain this?

"Are the carriers a *real* people?" I ask him.

"Yes, of course," says Ned.

"What kind of people?" asks Maya.

"Normal people," says Ned. "For the most part."

"Letter carriers, Ned?" I ask.

"Hmmm? No, no, no. They're a First Nations tribe living in northern British Columbia. They got the name because they carried the ashes of their dead relatives a long way in some kind of pack on their backs. Didn't I already tell you all this?"

We shake our heads no. He is looking at us through the rearview mirror.

Ahead are a diner and a gas station. Ned surprises us by pulling in. We have almost a full tank of gas and we do not eat out as a rule; it is cheaper to picnic in the car, buying groceries in large discount grocery stores when we can find them.

Ned turns off the engine. "Who's hungry?"

The boys yip. They are always hungry. I am dying for a hot meal. My mother gives Ned a look that says, Can we afford this? but he ignores her and shepherds us inside, where the waitress puts a pot of coffee and two cups in front of Ned and my mother without even asking.

"Thanks," says Ned with some surprise in his voice.

"It's a long ways down the road before you get to anything. No one comes in here but doesn't want coffee. I always bring it first thing."

"How do you know which way we're going?" asks Ned.

"Don't matter," says the waitress. "It's a long ways either direction. The world just kind of happened in other places and left us alone. But I got a sister moved to Regina and she says development is such that ain't no place going to be lonely much longer.

So many people multiplying so fast, we're going to be like ants in an anthill someday."

"Well," says my mother. "You couldn't tell from the look of things around *here*."

The woman looks out the window. There's a long lone wintry aspect, with nothing really to see but a few frosty tussocks now and again. But she looks as if she expects the answer to the future to be down the road somewhere. Or as if maybe while she was serving someone eggs, she missed the condos going up on the horizon. She scans it. No, nothing there, as usual; then her eyes scan further than that. So much further they must be going beyond the now and into the past or the future.

"Well," she says slowly. "I suspect it will happen in my children's time."

"How many children do you have?" asks my mother.

"None," says the woman, and keeps chewing her gum as if she hasn't said anything strange. She must be fifty at least. When does she plan to have these children?

"Well!" says Ned. "Menus?"

She puts red padded menus in front of all of us. "I'll be back in a bit."

"Thank you," says my mother.

"I want a burger and fries," says Max.

"I don't know if they make those at ten a.m., Max," says my mother.

"Chet'll make anything. He don't care," says the waitress, who is taking an order a few tables away but seems to monitor all conversations. Maybe it's a godlike talent she's developed in this lone diner in this lone expanse of prairie. She might be well known, put on exhibit, worshipped and revered or at least pretty well respected if she weren't here in the middle of the unknown. Unknown herself. A person who can hear all conversations at once. Here in this pocket of strangeness where there aren't enough souls to compare her to, or people to find out about her.

The waitress keeps talking to us while writing the other people's orders. "Burger and fries is a real good choice. Chet don't make anything fit to eat 'cept that. You wouldn't think someone could screw up an egg but he manages it."

We all close our menus and stare out the window, looking off at the view she faces all day every day. Each of us conjuring up our own vision of the future on that blank gray horizon. Or maybe the others just deciding on the hamburger and fries or French toast. You can only guess at other people's thoughts. I always assume they are lost in the same strange tangle of ideas I am having, trying to solve the puzzling universe. But half the time, if asked, they say they're not thinking anything much at all.

She comes back and we order burgers and fries. When the food sits steaming in front of us it is heavenly.

"How come burger and fries from a flat grill like they have in these places always tastes so much better?" I ask my mother.

The waitress is wiping off a table a couple of booths away but answers without looking up. "It's because all the other things that gets cooked on that grill flavors the meat. Chet don't never wash the grill. Good fry cooks never do."

We eat in silence. It's not every day you get a waitress who explains the future and the mystery of diner hamburgers to you in the same morning.

"Well, I guess it's about time I did," says Ned, as if our minds have all been psychically connecting

in the car and we can so easily pick up the thread
of his thoughts.

"Did what?" I ask, eating French fries with vo-
luptuous pleasure. Why is ketchup always so much
better out of a red squeeze bottle? I want one for
our house but I know somehow that it wouldn't be
the same.

"Did tell you about the Carriers. About how I
met Mary." He begins, "One summer when I was
in college—"

"Which college?" interrupts Maya. She likes her
details precise.

"Uh, I don't remember which it was, but one of
them," he says.

"How many did you go to?" I ask.

"Oh, quite a few, Bibles, quite a few."

"Which one did you *graduate* from?" I ask.

"Well, technically speaking, none."

"You didn't graduate?" I ask. "Then how could
you have an MA?"

"Signs and wonders, Bibles."

"I don't know what that means," I say.

"Nobody knows what it means," he says. "Anyhow, not relevant to my story. I was having some

trouble finding summer employment and I saw an ad for a firewatcher."

"What's that?" asks Hershel.

"I didn't know either when I first read the ad, Hershel. But later I found out it's a person who sits in this great tall tower on a mountaintop in the middle of the woods, which in British Columbia means the middle of nowhere at all. Or, as I began to think as I sat there in that tower every day watching the sun come up one way and go down another, the middle of everywhere, the very middle of everywhere."

"I don't know what you mean," says Hershel. Ned never gets tired of explaining things to them or even reexplaining endlessly if they forget or weren't paying attention the first time.

"Yes, you do, Hershel," says my mother. "Think of sitting on the porch steps back home and watching the ocean at sunset and sunrise. Do you remember that?"

Hershel nods.

"Well, didn't you think you were in the very center of the universe then? Didn't we all?"

"I don't know," says Hershel, and squirts ketchup

from the red squeeze bottle all over his plate. He
has lost interest. You can never get too abstract
with him. He isn't made for it.

My mother smiles. Ned smiles. I don't know if it
is at Hershel or if they are remembering sitting on
the porch, watching the waves.

I am thinking that we would go through a lot of
ketchup if we got a red squeeze bottle. Max and
Hershel have squirted out way more than they are
going to use. I am also thinking that my mother
doesn't seem to realize that the center of the universe for Max and Hershel has become the endless
grasslands but I do not want to be the one to pro-
vide her with this worrying detail.

"Anyhow, Hershel, they dropped me at this big
tower, like a big castle turret with a little apartment up at the top. They had to helicopter me in
because I was so far north into the mountains that
there were no roads. And I sat there all summer
and watched for fires."

"Did you put them out?" asks Max.

"No, Max, they didn't expect me to put out any
fires, just spot them. It was very lonely work, as
you can imagine. And after a few weeks I got

bored, so even though I had been warned not to, I decided to go for a walk in the woods. Among other things, I needed to stretch my legs. That was my undoing. The need for exercise," says Ned.

"Why did they tell you not to take a walk?" asks Max.

"Because in those deep forests with trees shooting up hundreds of feet overhead, where you can't see a horizon, there are no trails, paths, markers, roads. And here's a tip for you, Max and Hershel. Every square inch of the forest looks like every other square inch. You *think* you can find your way back to the fire tower, easy as anything, by recognizing landmarks, a creek here, an oddly shaped tree there. But the thing is that before you know it you are going in circles. And then when you find a creek, well, which way along the creek did you come? *All* the trees now look kind of oddly shaped. And six hours later you realize you may be miles from your starting point. There's no way of knowing. Should you keep going forward and possibly take yourself still farther away? If you stop no one will come for you. It may be days before the rangers realize you aren't answering your phone and send someone to look for you. Do you know how hard it is to see someone through those trees? By the time you understand you've done a stupid thing, it's too late. So here's my advice. If you ever take a job as a firewatcher, do not go for a walk in the woods."

Max and Hershel are nodding earnestly. My mother looks at them and says, "Oh, but, Ned, you're here now. You must have gotten out of those woods *somehow*."

"Well, yes, Felicity, but the moral of the story remains the same."

"Don't go for a walk in the woods, Hershel," says Max, nodding his head at him. They stare solemnly at each other. Since my mother married Ned, factions have formed. Maya and I. Max and Hershel. Ned and my mother. Subsets. Of course, there are others too. Ned and I have our own subset built on the understanding of adventures and the lure of outlaw life. I think I am more of an adventurer and Ned is more of an outlaw and there seems to be a difference I can't quite put my finger on.

I would like to figure this out but I am too

distracted now by Hershel and Max manically nodding to each other. They worship the ground Ned walks on. As long as he is around to explain the universe to them they are perfectly content and I wonder if we are all looking for that, someone to explain the universe satisfactorily to us. Will they keep his explanations as truth all their lives or will they grow up and move beyond them? Will they go through their whole lives afraid to walk in the woods or will they grow up and think that Ned knew no more than anyone else? And he couldn't speak French.

"I won't," says Hershel solemnly back to Max, and they both nod again. "I won't ever go for a walk in the woods."

"So there I am, lost in the wild, the sun beginning to set," says Ned, happy that all eyes are on him now, as if watching him going through the forest. "Which would be helpful if I knew if the tower was north, south, east or west of me, but I don't. I just keep walking. I don't know what else to do. It's very hard to sit still when you're that agitated. And I am mad at myself for being such a fool. I spend a lot of time trying to decide whether

I would rather be eaten by a bear or a wolf. Bear or wolf, I keep asking myself, bear or wolf?"

"Which did you decide?" asks Max.

"Bear. Because wolves hunt in packs and they're smart. Smart is scarier than big. And a wolf will circle you and then while you have your eye on it, the rest of the pack will race out of nowhere from six different directions to surround you and rip you to pieces."

"That's nonsense," says Maya. "There are no such things as wolves anymore. Only in fairy tales."

"Just because they're in fairy tales doesn't mean they're *just* in fairy tales, Maya," I say. "Just because they don't live in Massachusetts or Saskatchewan doesn't mean they don't *exist*."

"Mrs. Gunderson says that lots of animals have become extinct in our lifetime."

"Well, as usual Mrs. Gunderson is absolutely right," says Ned. "But wolves are not yet extinct."

"Did you see any?" asks Maya.

"No," says Ned.

"Then how do you know? Probably something you imagined. Because you were afraid. Mrs. Gunderson says we often imagine things when we're afraid."

"I bet even Mrs. Gunderson knows that wolves are real," I say. Why do I even bother arguing? Already Maya is frowning, framing an argument.

Ned leaps in quickly. "Well, anyway, Mayie." He's the only one to call Maya Mayie and only when he's afraid of her. She gets this vertical wrinkle on her forehead that portends approaching storms. It is there now. "I was definitely scared. We can all agree on that. But I kept walking because there was no sense just waiting around for the Welcome Wagon."

"What's the Welcome Wagon?" asks Hershel.

"It's a big red wagon that welcomes you," says Maya.

"Exactly," says Ned, who has given up correcting her. It is one thing for me to enjoy Maya's Mrs. Gundersonland but I think it would behoove a grown-up to set her straight. "Anyhow, night is falling and I'm getting cold and even squirrels begin to sound ominously large and menacing as they snap twigs and scurry up trees. Then I hear it. A big sound."

Ned takes a bite of burger.

"How big?" asks Hershel.

"Oh, big!" says Ned. "Not squirrel-size, that's for

darn sure. I am hoping it's a moose. Moose are sweet and shy. Moose can be avoided—unlike charging bears. Have you ever seen a moose run?"

He looks at Max and Hershel, waiting for an answer, but really, where would they have seen a running moose in their short little lives? They confirm that they have seen no running moose, so thankfully we can get on with the story. "Well, they look like their legs aren't connected to their bodies. Everything appears to be sort of shaken loose in a moose."

"Are you trying to rhyme?" asks Maya.

"No, ma'am, it happened quite by accident," says Ned. "Anyhow, moose, I'm pretty sure, are vegetarians. But it isn't a moose."

He stops and looks at us as if the horror of this is just occurring to him for the first time. He is all surprise. Ned is the master of suspense. I like Ned's stories but the suspenseful pauses can be held until I forsake all hope of sanity. I have learned that the best way to speed things along is to display no interest during the pauses. Maya has learned this too. We look at each other and go back to eating our burgers with no apparent curiosity about what is coming out of the woods. But it does no good because Max and Hershel, as usual, hang on Ned's every word.

"What is it?" asks Hershel.

"Not bear or wolf or moose," says Ned.

"ALIENS!" says Hershel.

Ned shakes his head no.

"Vikings!" says Max. Ned has a Viking bone that he takes out periodically so he and Hershel and Max can wonder over it all over again.

"Frogs!" says Hershel.

"Not alien, Viking, dog or frog, moose or goose," I prompt him.

"Oh, for heaven's sakes," Maya says crabbily. "Will everyone please stop rhyming?"

"It was a man," says Ned, looking nervously at Maya. "A Native man. He was carrying some rabbits he'd shot and was on his way home."

"He killed bunnies?" asks Maya.

"These weren't petting bunnies, Maya, these were eating bunnies," says Ned.

"What's the difference?" asks Maya.

"Some spent shotgun shells," admits Ned. "Anyhow, he took me with him. He even had cigarettes."

Ned looks blissful at the memory. "He brought me back to his village, where they let me bunk down with them. They had traplines and were netting fish and trapping animals and hunting from their summer camp. They didn't mind or care or even question my sudden appearance but just sort of moved over and made room for me. That's where I met Mary. She had an extra room in her cabin and she made a bed for me there. It was my first introduction to the Carrier people. Their whole way of life fascinated me. I learned to hunt with the men. The women smoked the fish and skinned and tanned the moose hides and cared for the children. They lived as they had for hundreds of years. I stayed on with them for a while."

"What happened to your job as a fire lookout?" I ask.

"Well, technically I couldn't return because I had no idea where that lookout tower was anymore. But to be honest, I didn't try very hard."

"But what if there had been a fire?" I ask.

"I knew that if I didn't check in, they'd phone me and if I didn't answer they would send the helicopter. I was more concerned about people fruitlessly searching for me, so I went into town and called them to let them know I was okay."

"Were they mad at you?" I ask.

"I suspect they were mostly glad that I was still alive. Otherwise it would have been tough recruiting the next guy. No one wants a job where the previous employee has disappeared."

The waitress is back and lays down the check. "Anything else?"

Ned looks at us but we shake our heads. I suspect we would all like a little pie but so it goes. Ned pays the bill and puts a toothpick in his mouth and we pile back into the car and hit the road.

"Have you even been in touch since then?" my mother asks Ned quietly as we drive along.

"No," says Ned. "That's the odd thing. I haven't talked to any of them in twenty years, so what in the world could have inspired Mary to suddenly remember me? I was just some kid who wandered into their camp, stayed awhile and wandered out."

"It's a mystery to be solved," I say. "Maybe, Ned, we should switch from outlaws to detectives."

"Maybe we could be outlaw detectives," says Ned. "Bandanas and fedoras."

"I still don't get why we are going at all," says Maya. "If you haven't even talked to her in twenty years. Couldn't you just phone her?"

"You don't just phone someone who is dying," I say to Maya. I don't actually know this but it is nice to be the expert for a change. I can change Gunderson to Fielding, my last name, and create my own Ms. Fieldingland.

"I owe her," says Ned to Maya. Then he goes back into his head, into the slumbering tangled thoughts of the road.

For a long time we drive in silence.

"Well," says my mother at last. The sun is at a springtime slant and the light is soaking into fields, filling them with energy. "Maybe the mountain passes won't be too difficult after all."

My mother has been a little worried about driving through the Rockies if the roads are icy.

"If the weather is nice maybe we'll get to your friend even sooner," says Maya. I think this is uncharacteristically considerate of Maya until she adds, "And we can leave sooner."

"Maybe," says Ned. The straight roads are giving way to curves as the prairies disappear and the land rises to its gently lifting hills.

My mother, who is looking dreamily on, murmurs, "But who can tell what's just around the bend?"

Some Amazing Things

Over the next two days the scenery changes. Where there has been flat land there are now mountains. Where there have been grasslands there are now woods. We go north, deeper into the trees, leaving civilization for longer and longer stretches of wilderness highway where the blackness of the forest is compensated for by the brilliance of the night sky. Stars reign here unquashed by human light. Birds' song breaks silence.

We have been driving a very long time on this stretch of tree-lined highway. At night the moon dangles tantalizingly at the end of the road as if it hangs just beyond the earth's edge. I imagine a highway that few know about that runs up to the

Yukon, then heads not just northward but upward to the moon. And the astronauts who set foot there find some old Chevys. Inside them are girls still in 1960s mod minidresses, pageboy haircuts and pink lipstick, and guys in bell-bottoms. Only very mod mods are daring and stylish enough to take the moon drive. But it's easier to find your way to the moon than back again and so they are stuck circling, the way Ned circled in the woods before a Carrier found him.

"Their clothes would be very out of date because there aren't many shopping malls on the moon," I say to Maya as I explain all this.

"How do they stay alive?" she asks skeptically. "If there are no grocery stores, what would they eat?"

"Green cheese," I say.

"Feh," she says. *Now* the idea is ridiculous.

"Moon milk," I say. I am quite taken by this idea.

"Moon milk." My mother has overheard. "Moon milk." Sometimes she just likes the sounds of words, the way sometimes she will stand very still, just liking the feel of the air. She used to do this in the soft warm boggy mudflats, when steam rose off the wet sand in little wisps. But I have seen her do it on the prairies as well, when arctic air was coming down to us from Russia and bathing us in stinging sprays of wind ice.

The car stops. We all sit there as if it will start again on its own.

Finally Max says, "The car stopped."

"It's out of gas," says Ned, and sighs. "We're fifty miles out of town and seventy-five or so from the Carrier camp and we're out of gas."

"How is that possible?" asks my mother.

"That's not possible but moon milk is?" says Maya in disgust.

"Hush, Maya, not now," says my mother. "What are we going to do?"

Ned heaves a huge sigh and opens the door. He walks around to my mother's window and signals for her to roll it down. "I'm going to hitchhike into the next town and get some gas and come back."

"Is that safe, Ned?" asks my mother.

"You have a better idea?" he asks. "I thought we could get through on our tank but I forget what rotten mileage this thing gets. I miscalculated." He sounds irritated. I think he blames himself but his tone is a warning not to say that we do too.

"Well!" says my mother. "That's what I thought too. That we'd be in town before the gas ran out."

"It's these darn northern roads. You forget they go on and on without even small towns or gas stations between," says Ned. Then when no one says anything, he sighs.

"All right," he says, sighing again, enormously this time, and he starts ambling away a bit from the car, his blue jeans frayed around the tops of his tennis shoes. There is a hole in the toe of one of them.

"Ned needs new tennis shoes," I say to my mother.

"I know," she says. "But he won't buy a pair unless he can find some that cost less than ten dollars like the ones he is wearing now."

"Did he buy them twenty years ago?" I say. "When tennis shoes cost that? It looks like it."

"I know," says my mother again. "But the quest for tennis shoes that cost less than ten dollars makes him happy."

"His toes are sticking out," says Maya.

"Cold but happy," I say to her.

Ned stands looking hopefully down the road for the longest time. The rest of us don't know what to do. It seems cruel to engage in anything while he waits there alone and yet we can't go out and stand with him or it will look like we want the passing car to pick us *all* up, which will certainly cut down on the chances of anyone stopping.

Finally a huge semi pulls to a noisy halt. It takes so long that Ned has to run up the road to get to it. He steps up to the window of the cab and leans in and then makes a thumbs-up gesture to us. He climbs in and that's the last we see of him for a while.

We sit still until all the car's heat is gone and we have to rely on our own. It is chilly but not the bitter cold of the prairies. There are buds on some trees, even on stretches dusted with snow. As if spring is putting out feelers, trying to find out if it's okay to emerge and show its face.

"I'm bored," says Maya.

"Let's get out!" yells Max.

"Let's take a walk," says my mother.

We leave the car and stroll down the road together.

"But not in the woods!" says Hershel. "Never in the woods. Never ever ever in the woods. Never in the woods."

"Never in the woods. Never in the woods," chants Max with him.

"Oh no," I say in low tones to Maya. "They're bored. Now they are going to be obnoxious. They will chant nonsense things endlessly and run around screaming."

"Good. Maybe it will keep the bears away," says Maya.

I glance at her with scorn but it startles my mother and she suddenly looks worried.

"I don't see any bears," I say to Maya.

"It doesn't mean they don't see *you*," she says.

I'll be glad when Maya finally has a friend. This constant sourness is wearing. But I know this isn't who she really is. She's just unhappy these days.

The boys want to get their trucks out of the car and run them down the road. My mother looks like she is about to protest the safety of this but a look in either direction tells us that we will not see a car for a long time and when we do, will have plenty of time to warn the boys.

My mother and Maya and I walk back and forth.
Mostly to keep warm.

"Listen to that bird, Jane," my mother says.
"What do you think it can be?"

We look up. It is an eagle but it is a sound all
wrong for an eagle. It makes me wonder if eagles
are all they're cracked up to be—if I've endowed
them with noble characteristics they entirely lack.
Perhaps they are cowardly whiny birds, burdened
with legendary qualities they never wanted to
assume.

Just then we hear the long slow clear call of a
wolf. It makes a tunnel through the air right to my
heart.

"That's it. Get in the car, all of you," says my
mother.

"There are no such things as wolves," says Maya
stoutly after we have stopped holding our breaths,
listening for the next howl. "It was probably a
dog."

"I love wolves," I say to her. "Only maybe not
too close to the car."

We sit there and shiver until Ned returns. He is
in a pickup truck with a large muscly young Native
man. Although snow is beginning to drift gently

down, the guy doesn't wear a coat. Flakes fall on his bare arms and he doesn't seem to notice. Perhaps because his arms are, as they appear, made of iron. He doesn't come to the car to meet us but he and Ned immediately open the gas cap and pour in gas from a can they take out of the back of the pickup.

My mother leaps out of the car and there is a lot of polite laughter and shaking of hands. Then Ned leads the man to the back window and motions for Hershel to roll it down. He introduces the man to us as Jim. Ned says he is a Carrier and is going to take us to the Carrier camp.

"Mary just got out of the hospital. Good timing," says Jim.

"That's wonderful," says my mother. "She's much better, then?"

"Nah, I think they just sent her to die at home," says Jim.

My mother looks startled.

Then, as if no one has any idea what to say next, the man takes the empty gas can and gets into his pickup and my mother and Ned jump back into the car to follow him.

My mother turns to see me staring at the muscly

man in the pickup and looks thoughtful, as if something new has just occurred to her. I don't want to be caught staring. For heaven's sake, I want to say, we've been sitting here with nothing but woods for what seems like forever. Sensorily deprived, really. I am suddenly disgusted with both my mother and Ned and the things they put us through sometimes. There really has not been enough privacy on this trip. I look stonily out the back window, embarrassed.

We drive right through the town. It takes about half a minute and then we are in pitch dark again going down the highway.

"If she's out of the hospital she must be functioning better," says my mother to Ned.

"Jim says she insisted on going home," says Ned. "She insists there's nothing much wrong with her. Anyhow, he says she's at least conscious now. But they all think she's going to die."

"So did they ask her why she kept calling your name?"

"He said they thought they'd let me ask her. In case it was personal."

"Did they tell her you were coming?"

"Yes."

"What did she say to that?"

"I don't know."

When we finally turn off the highway, night has placed us deeply and darkly into the universe. Every star sits millimeters from every other so that the sky is a dome of pinpricks of light.

"Oh man," says Ned as we drive a little ways down what appears to be an old logging road. The road stops abruptly and we are left with just woods. "Now I remember this place. This road. I remember the way everything smells like pine. Oh man, I love this smell. Bibles, this is the best smell in the world."

But he is wrong. The best smell in the world is low tide and the slightly musty smell of our house on the beach.

"Where's the village?" asks my mother in confusion.

"Down a path. We have kind of a long walk. I'm sorry. I can carry Max. Do you think you can take Hershel that far? It's about a mile or so in."

"I think so," says my mother but she doesn't sound happy. Long gone are the days when she could carry either of them easily. They are both asleep in the back. "Jane, can you take the red suitcase? It's got everyone's pajamas."

"Where are we sleeping?" asks Maya.

"No one knows, it's an adventure, Mayie," says Ned.

I grab the red suitcase and get out. I yawn. The earth is wet and there is a rich damp mossy smell. Jim comes back to us from where he parked his pickup. He takes the suitcase out of my hands and I'm glad. I'm really tired now and don't feel like carrying it through the woods in the dark. To be honest, as much as I want adventures, tonight is not the night for them. I think of my bed back in Massachusetts with its old Pendleton blanket, the dotted swiss curtains, my favorite star.

Jim has a flashlight and walks ahead of us shining a path, which is actually kind of useless as it illuminates the earth for him but not for us in the back. I trip on tree roots from time to time. I am surprised that Maya doesn't whine but perhaps she is inhibited by Jim.

Finally we get to a clearing. There are a lot of cabins with smoke coming out of their chimneys. The woodsmoke has a thick pleasant smell.

Jim goes to check on Mary but reports that she is asleep.

"I can wake her," he says uncertainly.

"Don't think of it," says my mother, and then there is an awkward pause.

"Why don't you sit down." He motions us to a fallen tree. "I just have to tell some people you are here."

We sit under the stars. It is much warmer than Saskatchewan. Maya clings to my mother's side. There are noises in the woods. Then we see a cabin door open and a family with startled and curious faces races out carrying bedding. It is obvious that Jim is clearing a cabin for us. This is uncomfortable but what can we do? We do not want to sleep in the car.

Jim stays awhile longer in the cabin and then another woman comes out, also throwing a curious squinty-eyed look at us although she can hardly make us out in the dark. I think we are the most exciting thing to happen here for a while.

There is no Walmart or roller rink or even movie theater for miles and miles. I bet they all get sick of each other's faces. This consoles me somewhat when Jim emerges and motions us over and says, "You can stay here."

"I hate to inconvenience those people," says my mother uncertainly.

"Oh no, they got plenty of room at her sister's place. They don't mind. They're glad you came to see Mary. People'd do just about anything for Mary." He shows us the cabin and says he will see us in the morning.

The cabin is warm. The beds look freshly made. I am hoping someone changed all the sheets. It is one thing to be outlaws. It is one thing to have adventures and recklessly take what comes. I am all for that but at the end of the day I want fresh linens.

My mother is looking at the beds. I bet she is thinking the same.

She heaves a sigh, unpacks and gets the boys into their pajamas. Maya and I change in the bathroom and I am glad to see that my mother has already put Hershel and Max in a small bed together. I will have a bed to myself.

In the close warm dark, with the sound of the fire, the crackling logs, the wind that whooshes through the pines and down the chimney, the spray of rain and ice against the roof in gusts, the sounds of movement outside, human or animal, impossible to tell, we lie content. Occasionally there is the soft sound of someone moving in his bed or a log shifting position. Quiet pockets of life in the still room. I think of the huge overarching starlit sky of the woods and wonder how it is to be up there in that great silence looking down at Earth. Maybe our explosions and tidal waves and wars are just quiet pockets of life in a larger still room.

I hear the howl of a wolf again. Thank goodness Maya is already gently snoring. Something primitive in me knows that it is safer to sleep huddled this way in one room at night with a fire. I wonder if my mother and Ned are asleep yet or if their thoughts fill this room with images the way mine do. I am at home here in a cabin. I would not know this if adventure had not led me here. It is not a place I would ever have thought to come on my own. Sometimes it is good to have things happen to you outside of your control. There are parts of yourself you would never discover otherwise. But sometimes it feels that in these new places, as much as I discover new parts of myself, I lose parts of the old Jane. The one who was safe and secure and happy on the beach.

Do my mother's thoughts and mine tangle in the night? Because I hear her gentle voice say, "Ned, sometimes at night I hear the sound of the ocean."

"That's the wind in the pines," he says practically, and I hear him roll over and start to snore.

··············

In the morning Jim takes us to see Mary. My mother wants Ned to go alone first but he wants to bring us all and introduce us. When we get inside her cabin it is dark and a little smoky and close. Perhaps they are keeping it extra warm because she is ill. She is a mass of gray hair on the bed looking exactly the color of one of the white charred logs in the fireplace. I wonder if when you live under these trees for so long you become partly tree. She turns a wrinkled tree bark face to us and then grins. She is missing quite a few key teeth. "NED!" she croaks.

"Hi, Mary," says Ned. He looks, all at once, shy.
"I wasn't sure you would recognize me."

"I didn't recognize you. I knew you were coming. You're changed now. You're old. Felicity, Hershel, Max, Maya and Jane." She says our names
while looking down the line at us.

I realize that Jim kept all our names straight
when he told her, which impresses me because he
only heard them once. I am thinking he is not only
brawny but very smart. It startles me that she calls
Ned old when she is so ancient herself. But maybe
when she saw him he was such a young man. Or
maybe she was trying to say older. She talks in a
halting way, needing large breaths to complete
sentences, straining as if afraid that any second she
will lose the ends of words.

"Whatcha doing here, Ned?" she asks. Then she
closes her eyes. As if she needs to rest after sentences too.

"They said when you were sick you kept calling
for me," says Ned.

"I don't remember. I don't remember the hospital much, Ned. Except the food. Bad food."

"Nobody likes hospital food," says my mother.
You can tell she is trying to find consoling things

to say. I think she would like to say consoling things to Ned too, this is so obviously hard for him. She rests her hand lightly on his upper arm.

"Are you in pain?" asks Ned. Somehow this seems kind of personal to me. He hasn't seen her in twenty years.

Mary shakes her head and then she lies back with her eyes closed and we all glance at each other. Now what?

"So you don't remember calling me?" Ned tries again.

Mary shakes her head.

"Oh."

It is hard to know where to go with this. I look at Maya anxiously. I am afraid she is going to burst out with some explosion about how we came all this way to see a dying person who doesn't know what we're doing here. But Maya is just looking cowed by circumstances. The boys are getting fidgety, though.

"Well, maybe I will take the boys outside," says my mother, but doesn't.

"Uh, I don't know what to say," says Ned. "I mean, I came because they said you called me."

"How many years has it been, Ned? Since you lived here."

"Oh, about twenty, I guess," says Ned. You can see everyone deflating. It is very hard to know how to feel when you've been feeling noble and now it turns out you've done a completely unnecessary thing and wasted a lot of gas to do it, not to mention tossed a family out of their nice warm cabin so you could sleep there.

"Twenty years," says Mary. "Goes by fast. But Jim told you . . ." She stops and breathes again loudly with a whispery sound as if her lungs are full of old paper.

Ned waits. We all wait. It seems the polite thing to do but she doesn't say anything and we get twitchy. You have no idea how long a few minutes can last until you have stood next to a dying woman politely waiting for her to finish her sentence.

Finally Ned says, "Jim told me what, Mary?"

"Jim told you . . . who . . . came to us," she gasps.

"Someone I know?" prompts Ned.

Mary nods and then there is another long wait

while she breathes her rattling breath. I am sorry but at this point I want to shout, What is this? Twenty questions?

We wait some more. Nobody even moves in case it distracts her.

"Who came to the camp?" asks Ned when it is clear Mary needs another prompt.

There is another long wait while she slowly opens her eyes. She shifts herself slightly upward on her pillows and looks into Ned's eyes for a long time before she says, "Your brother."

Back on the Road

Well, that's a conversation stopper, as you can imagine. Finally Ned says, "My *brother?*"

Then Mary croaks, "Your *brother.*"

Then Ned looks astounded again and says, "My *brother?*"

Then Mary says, "Your *brother!*"

They go around a few times this way with long pauses between question and answer as Mary gathers her strength to speak again. I am worried she will use up all her energy on this one answer and we'll never find out anything else. My mother must be worried about this too because she suddenly leaps in and asks, "*Which* brother, Mary?"

"Yeah!" says Ned. "Which brother?"

"Says his name is John," says Mary. She is paling with the effort of the interview and my mother, Ned and I all have our hands clasped, hoping we will get the end of the story before she expires into sleep . . . or *worse.*

"*John?*" asks Ned.

"John," says Mary, but it is unclear if she is confirming or just repeating.

"*John?*" says Ned.

"Can we go out and play with our trucks?" asks Hershel.

This draws Mary's attention to him for the first time and she turns her head and looks straight at him as she says, "The *Amazing* John!"

This freaks out the usually unflappable Hershel, who takes two steps back.

"What's amazing about him?" asks Ned.

"No, no, his name . . . ," says Mary. Her voice becomes thinner and reedier. She is definitely losing lung power now.

"Yes," says Ned, encouragingly, "John is his name."

"No . . . ," says Mary, her hands clenching with the effort, "Amazing . . ."

"John is amazing?" asks Ned.

"No, Ned," says my mother. "I think she is saying 'Amazing' is part of his name."

Mary nods emphatically or clearly means to although actually it's just a limp neck bend.

"The Amazing John?" asks Ned.

Mary nods again but this time the movement
is barely discernible. "John the Amazing," she
croaks.

"What kind of a crackpot name is that?" asks
Ned in normal tones and not the hushed reveren-
tial ones we use for the sick and dying.

"Well, a stage name, maybe, Ned," says my
mother helpfully.

Mary nods again. She opens her eyes. You can
tell she is gathering strength for the home stretch.
"Vegas," she whispers.

"John has an *act in Vegas*?" asks Ned.

"Magician," says Mary.

"John is a *magician*?" says Ned. "But he was never
any good with his hands!"

Mary just stares at Ned. And really, I think, weak
or not, there is no other appropriate reaction. After all, what is she supposed to do—John is Ned's
silly family, it's got nothing to do with her.

"Well!" says Ned when it is apparent he is getting

no help with this. He sits down in a chair next to her bed.

My mother takes the boys outside. How can she stand to leave at this most interesting moment? But I guess that is what it is to be a mother. Max has had to have a dreamcatcher taken from him and Hershel, it turns out, has been busy shredding a corner of the blanket where a thread is loose. Duty calls.

"Did he say what he was doing here?" asks Ned.

"Looking for you. Under bed." Mary's eyes are closed again.

"He was looking for me under the bed?" asks Ned. Talk about amazing!

But Mary just jabs downward with one birdclaw hand. I look down. There's a small duffel bag poking out from underneath. I pick it up. Mary nods at me.

"Left for you," she says, and closes her eyes again as if mission accomplished.

"John came? He left this *bag* for me?" Ned looks astounded but Mary doesn't bother answering. Ned takes the bag, stupefied.

"Open it," I urge.

"Yeah," he says, shaking himself like a dog. "Right."

He opens the duffel bag.

It is full of money.

＊＊＊

We are back in the car driving south.

"And another thing," says Ned, "Jim says John was heading north briefly before returning to Vegas. *NORTH!* What the heck is north of B.C.? Tundra? Ice floes? He was heading toward an ice floe, taking time off to drop a bag of money in the woods? Does that sound on the up-and-up to you? Does that even remotely make sense? And how the heck would he even find the Carriers?"

"*You* found them," I say.

"Yeah, but I wasn't *looking* for them," says Ned.

"So, it must be even easier to find them if you are," I insist. "What I can't figure out is why he thought you would be there again. I mean, he knew you left years ago."

"Unless he wasn't really looking for me, he was

looking for a remote safe place to drop a bag of money."

"If all you want is somewhere to hide something then there's got to be more convenient remote places than northern B.C. If you don't think John is capable of larceny then there must be another explanation," says my mother.

"I don't know. People change. People grow old, people die, people get scared, people go away, people have kids, people don't. All kinds of things change them."

"Maybe he was going on vacation," says my mother.

"What kind of vacation?" says Ned in skeptical tones.

My mother thinks for a moment. "A cruise!"

"A cruise?"

"People go on those Alaskan cruises. I think they leave from British Columbia."

"On the coast. He wasn't on the coast."

"Maybe he was making his way to the coast."

But Ned goes on as if he hasn't listened to a word she's said. "Well, I don't even know what I'm supposed to *think* about this. I don't know what I'm supposed to *do* with it. This is a lot of money! And I'll tell you another thing, I want nothing to do with it. It's going back to John."

"Are we going to have to go *somewhere else* to find your brother before we can go home?" asks Maya in very cranky tones.

"I don't know," says Ned.

My mother turns to address Maya, who is turning around to face her. "We're going to do whatever we have to, Maya. We're a family now and Ned's family is our family too."

My mother is keeping this chirpy and cheerful but I see something in her eyes. Some foreboding. Some glimmer that we are heading south and it will be a long time before fate takes us east and back home.

The Wild West

Nobody really likes Nevada.

We have had a long trip down through Washington and Oregon. Through many different landscapes that didn't quite jibe with the Outlaw Adventures, as I have come to think of them. But when we hit Nevada we hit the Wild West. Now we are talking. There are *tumbleweeds*. It is a horrible place, really. Perfect!

At a gas station outside of some small town, while my mother and Maya use the restroom and Hershel and Max pick out a chocolate bar, I say to Ned, "We're real outlaws now, with a bag of ill-gotten gains in a vast forlorn dangerous deadly snake-ridden moonscape. Isn't this cool?"

"Not so cool, Bibles, not so cool," he says. He is already peeling the paper off a Nestlé Crunch bar. The candy bar decision is never a long debate for Ned. He just grabs the first one he sees. I think this is very telling but I'm not sure exactly what it tells.

"How do you pick a candy bar so fast?" I ask, thinking out loud. "It takes me forever to decide whether I want a Snickers or a PayDay."

"First off, never get the PayDay," says Ned.

The thing about having two adults in the family now is that you get a whole other frame of reference. My mother would never be able to pontificate on candy bar selection.

"I like nuts," I say.

"Yes. But nuts are optional, unlike chocolate. What is the point of a chocolate bar without chocolate?" asks Ned.

"We could buy a lot of candy bars with our outlaw money." I keep hoping to rekindle his excitement. Ever since we left the Carriers he has looked haunted more than wild and free and roguish.

"This is a bag of *real* money, Jane," he says. "I don't want to play games with this. I certainly don't want to spend it all on chocolate bars. I just want to return it and go back to Massachusetts like we promised your mom, okay?"

Suddenly the guy behind the cash register looks real interested.

"Pick a candy bar, Jane!" says Ned.

I startle. He usually doesn't call me Jane unless he's irritated with me. So I grab a Three Musketeers, which I don't even like, which goes to show that his technique of snatching the first one at hand doesn't work for everyone, and he pays for all four candy bars and hustles us outside.

I peer at him questioningly and he relents. "Look, I just wish I knew more about this money. You understand I haven't spoken to anyone in my family for twenty years? I don't even know where they are anymore. And now I find myself carrying money that came from who knows where. And why was John going north of northern B.C.? The whole thing makes no sense."

"But I like it," I say. "It's an adventure. It's an *outlaw* adventure."

"Well, it makes *me* nervous," says Ned.

"Does it make Mom nervous?" I ask.

"Sometimes I think nothing makes your mother

nervous," says Ned, and just then my mother and Maya come out of the washroom. They see us eating candy bars and go inside to get a couple for themselves with Ned's toes tapping.

"You sure are fidgety," I say.

"Did you see that cashier's ears perk up when you mentioned a bag of money?"

"Oh, you're just being paranoid," I say.

"Uh-huh," he says in an unconvinced voice, and gets the boys into the car and buckled in so we can set off the second my mother and Maya return.

"I think you ought to try deep breathing," I say when we are rolling along again. "Although don't do it too obviously or no one will take you seriously as an outlaw."

"Why should Ned try deep breathing?" asks my mother.

"Jane thinks I'm too nervous," says Ned.

"Oh well, I suppose we're all a little nervous . . . ," says my mother vaguely. She is leafing through the Nevada guidebook she bought at the gas station. Now she looks up and points out the window into the scrubby desert. "Look at that! Wild burros!" She finds the section about them and reads it. Hershel and Max are leaping up and down in their seats even though my mother is the only one who saw the burros because we are whizzing by so fast.

"Should I turn around and see if we can find them again?" asks Ned, but he looks pale and strained. His neck muscles are tight and corded.

My mother glances over at him. "Don't bother," she says. "I'm sure we'll see more."

Then everyone goes back to reading or playing games or trying to grab my feet and beautify them and it is quiet the rest of the way to Reno.

Reno is full of casinos. We come in as the light is fading and the bright casino bulbs shatter twilight.

Money is what a lot of people seem to think about in Nevada. Ned explains that people rarely win at gambling. That some win but mostly the casinos know they will always take more money than they lose. I don't understand how this works but if it is true I feel sorry for all these gamblers who don't seem to know this.

The first hotel we stay in in Nevada is a casino in Reno. To get to the elevator you have to pass this big dark gambling place full of mirrors and

flashing lights and slot machines. It is very disorienting. I think if people come to this place on
purpose they must be trying to disappear because
when you are inside it, it is as if no part of your life
has ever existed. There seems no way out to your
future, your past is not here, all there is is the dark
present with the flashing lights and the money going clink clank clunk. John has chosen to live in
Nevada. Is it just because that's where he could
make a living as a magician or does he like it? I
want to ask him when we see him but I don't know
how to do it without sounding rude.

The next morning we leave Reno at the crack of
dawn.

On the way down to Las Vegas we barely
pass another car except when we come to small
towns and sometimes not even then. We see large
military installations and what I now know to
be legal whorehouses because I asked Ned what
all the double-wides with names like Cat House
were and he explained it at the next rest stop.
Maya is furious with Ned for not telling her and I
want to but it would mean having to explain so
much else.

Finally, when she won't leave me alone, I just say to her, "It's for ladies of the night, okay?"

"Oh," she snorts. "Ladies who only come out at night. More fairy tales." She and Mrs. Gunderson are having a good snort over that.

For no reason I can figure out this makes me furious. That she can be so contentedly wrong because she has such preconceived notions about everything.

"You know, you'd better stop having such a closed mind, Maya," I say. "You'd better stop assuming you know everything or you'll be ignorant your whole life."

"Then tell me what a lady of the night is," says Maya.

We go round and round with this all the way to Las Vegas and I wish I had kept my mouth shut. Meanwhile my mother keeps spotting burros, always with the thrill of the first time, and Hershel wants to know if the military installations are alien camps. Ned has made the mistake of telling him that this highway is called the Extraterrestrial Highway because so many UFOs are seen here. Max wants to know if there are Viking bones. Ned

says no, but probably Indian bones and wild mus-
tang bones and maybe even extraterrestrial bones.
Max says he's only interested in Vikings.

"Outlaw bones!" suggests Ned, but it has the
ring of desperation.

"Give it up," I advise, and settle back to take a
nap. These days sleep is the only privacy I get.

When we get to Las Vegas we stay in a crummy
motel with a swimming pool, on the outskirts of
town. My mother elects to hang out with Hershel
and Maya and Max around the pool all day while
Ned and I go into town and look for John the
Amazing.

"This is a good adventure," I say to Ned when
we arrive downtown. "It's like a treasure hunt. Or
being detectives."

"Um-hmm," says Ned as we drive down the
Strip. He doesn't look as excited about it as I am.
We are looking to see if we can find anything indi-
cating where John the Amazing is working but of
course we can't. He is small potatoes, says Ned.

Who would put his name up on a billboard? We will have to park and get a newspaper.

But after we park we are ravenous. We go into one of the casino buffets for lunch. I have never seen so much food in my life. It is a football field of food. It is dark and cavernous and disorienting like the casinos but instead of taking your money they take your hunger. Instead of want want want, it is too much too much too much. Maybe it is supposed to balance out, all the food they shove into you, all the money they take out of you. Maybe they want to fill you so full of food that in a stupor you will wander upstairs and throw all your quarters into the nearest slot, unable to stagger to the next casino down the road.

We eat until we are ready to fall over, as designed, but foil their little plan by going right past the slots and into the bright light of midday.

"Now all I want to do is nap," says Ned as we waddle out.

"Me too," I say. "And we still haven't found John."

We pick up a newspaper but can't find any ads for him so Ned suggests we walk around and check out casinos and see if anyone has heard of him. We do this for a while but it is hot and crowded and everyone is having a good time but us, and finally it is getting close to dinner.

"I don't have a clue what to do now," says Ned. He sounds so dispirited and disappointed that I feel bad for him. Is he sad because he wants to get rid of this money or because he wants to see his brother? It's hard to get a fix on how Ned feels about his family. He never talks about them.

We get into the car and start to head back to the motel but there is a traffic jam and so Ned swears in his newly minted language, "Oh shuckserooni." However, he puts enough venom into such a horrible corny word that he makes it respectably biting.

As soon as we get to an intersection, he turns.

"What are you doing?" I ask mildly, the tires squealing as he makes the quick tight turn.

"Trying to avoid this mess," he says. "We could be stuck here forever."

"Do you know where you're going?" I ask.

"No," he barks. We are both tired, footsore and sweaty. We really need water but we thought we'd be at the motel relatively quickly. The car has no air-conditioning and it's blasting hot. This was not so bad on the highway with windows open, but sitting in traffic with the sun beating down and the honking and roar of idling engines, it is horrible. It is causing Ned's brain to melt. He is making bad decisions. He keeps deciding there are even quicker shortcuts and turns this way and that until we are completely lost.

"Go to a gas station and get a map," I say.

"Bibles, sometimes I wish you'd just sh—" he begins, when I interrupt him by shrieking. He pulls the car to a skidding halt.

"What? What!" he says, looking frantic.

I point out the window.

"Bibles, don't you EVER do that to me in traffic again," he says, but then sees what I see. On a sign in front of a crummy run-down old casino, black letters, some of them missing and askew, read JOHN HE AMA ING.

Ned and I Hit a Saloon

Ned leans his head on the steering wheel, with both hands still clutching the top of it. I notice that the back of his neck is red and sweaty.

"Well," he says finally, lifting his head. "Let's go in."

"Yes," I say, suddenly getting a second wind. "Let's."

We park and get out and head toward the front door. "The universe led us here! This is enough to make you believe in Nellie Phipps," I say to him. Nellie was the preacher I had had real and fake mystic adventures with in Massachusetts. It had been hard to tell which were which and I'd sworn never to believe in anything again. Yet here we were, by great coincidence, where John worked. What were the odds?

"Just do me a favor and don't pass out any Bibles," teases Ned. Sometimes all it takes to restore someone's good humor is the universe doing him a little favor for a change. Making things a little easier. Letting him know it's on his side, despite former evidence to the contrary.

"Listen," says Ned as he holds the door open for me. "I'm sorry about saying 'Shhh' before."

"You were going to say 'Shut up,'" I point out matter-of-factly.

"I was not!"

"You were too!"

"Wasn't!"

"Was."

"Yeah, whatever," says Ned. Now he is casing the joint and doesn't appear to remember what we are talking about. He has forgotten me already with the nervousness about the new task at hand. We are going to see his brother.

There is a woman behind the bar, with a long nose and a lot of blond hair piled on her head. She is wearing a spangled shirt that is low-cut and doesn't seem to me to be proper afternoon wear. I think it should be more of an evening thing. She has long dangling earrings and is chewing gum.

"Hiya," she says to Ned. "What'll you have?"

"Well, actually," says Ned, and he pauses like he doesn't know what to say next. "I'm just looking for John."

"John who?" asks the woman, her charming tight smile falling into slack boredom.

"John the Amazing?" says Ned.

"He doesn't go on until eight tonight, honey," she says. "Why don't you have a drink in the meantime."

I look at her in disbelief. It is only four o'clock. He would have to have a lot of drinks if the meantime is four hours. And doesn't she see me standing there? Is it really her intention to contribute to the delinquency of a minor? I squint my eyes and try to look bored too. Even more bored than she is. Like she may be bored in this crummy bar in this crummy casino on the outskirts of nowhere but I'm even more bored because I've been directly to somewhere and back and there's not much you can't show me.

"I don't want to see the show. I need to *talk* to him," says Ned. His voice goes up a quarter pitch. Sometimes it does that when he is nervous. It is not his best feature.

"Why?" she asks.

"Why what?" asks Ned.

"Why'd you want to see him?"

"He's my *brother*," says Ned.

"Says *who*?" says the woman.

Ned pulls out his wallet and shows her his driver's license. "See, same last name."

She stares at it for a long time and then looks at him flatly and says, "I don't know his last name."

I snort. She gives me the same flat look.

"Well, is he around or not?" asks Ned.

"I dunno. Ask Gary," says the woman, and turns to serve someone else.

"Where's Gary?" asks Ned.

But the woman ignores him so Ned and I go to find someone else we can ask. We finally find a guy cleaning a bathroom and ask him but he shrugs. He doesn't seem to speak English. There are people gambling all around the room and Ned says there must be security somewhere and we can ask *them*. He finally accosts a big hulking guy in a suit who is clearly patrolling the joint. The guy looks at Ned and says, "Why'd you want to know?"

"He's my *brother*," says Ned a little too loudly. I don't think he should be loud with this guy. You can see his muscles under his suit. Ned seems to have no instinct about who to get tough with and who to get whiny with. I could handle this much better but I know he won't let me be the spokesman.

"Who says?"

"Look, I just want to see him. Is he around?"

"Yeah, he's around somewhere but I don't know where and I'm not going to look for him for you. Why don't you come back at showtime? He usually turns up for that."

Ned whips about and heads for the casino door. I follow him, trying to present a sympathetic demeanor.

"Oh Christ, Bibles, I wish I had a cigarette," says Ned when we get outside.

"*Usually?*" I say.

"Huh?" says Ned, blinking in the dazed way you do when you come out of these dark caves.

"*Usually* turns up for his show?"

"Oh yeah. I caught that too."

"So what do you want to do?" I ask Ned.

"I dunno. Go to the motel and come back for the show, I guess. Maybe we can all go. I bet the boys would like a magic show."

But when we tell my mother she says Max and Hershel are done in. They have been swimming all afternoon in the motel pool and she doesn't think they will last that long. Maya is watching television. We didn't have a television in Saskatchewan or Massachusetts, and she is transfixed.

Ned looks at her sitting glued to something inane with a laugh track and says, "Don't you want to see a live magic show, Mayie?"

"No," she says without taking her eyes from the screen.

"Come on," I say. "It will be fun. The magician is Ned's *brother.*"

"I want to stay in bed and watch TV," she says.

"*All night?*" I ask. "Mama is going to make you turn it off when the boys go to bed anyhow."

"Then I'll watch in the other room."

We have taken two motel rooms.

"Mama isn't going to let you stay in a motel

room alone," I say. "Which means you'll have nothing to do when the boys go to bed except read."

"Be quiet, I can't hear," says Maya.

Ned and I shrug. Ned says he will go pick up
dinner from Burger King for us. My mother says
this is the last fast-food dinner we are going to
have for a while.

"I feel positively toxic," she says.

"It's hard to eat on the road," says Ned.

"It's hard to eat decently on the road," she
agrees.

"Don't forget the toys," says Max.

"Yeah, don't forget the toys," says Hershel. They
mean the free toys you get with a children's meal.
So Ned takes them with him while I go for a swim
and change into my best jeans and a nice shirt.
I want to look presentable if we are going to a
theater.

My mother does a little yoga in a corner of the
room and then we sit on a couple of hard metal
chairs in front of the motel and watch the sun drop
over the desert. The edge of the horizon is almost
cruelly sharp here, the land flat, chalky and jagged. But now at twilight the light changes it so

that it softens, its edges rounding slightly, blurring into pale orange and rose and peach. It mellows even the hardest aspect of the desert, its giant cacti and stones and snakes. It makes you realize that even in the places that look most formidable, there is a great and gentle beauty with no thought to forward or backward, past, present, good, bad, should or shouldn't. I mention this to my mother and she gazes out and nods.

"Maya is watching a lot of TV," I say.

"Well, it's short-lived because we don't have a TV at home," my mother says practically.

I don't say anything. My mother smiles and puts a hand on my forearm. "Maya is fine, Jane. Maya is just impatient to go home and it's making her cranky."

Then the boys return. We can tell it is them a block away because Ned is letting them hang their heads out the window and scream into the wind. My mother never lets them do this because it is dangerous and they might get their heads lopped off. When we get to the car they have their seat belts on and are sitting like perfect gentlemen. I would think I had been mistaken about the

screaming except that they are a little too perfect.
The hands folded in the laps is the giveaway.

"Was that you screaming?" I ask Max.

"No," says Max solemnly.

"No," says Hershel.

I roll my eyes.

Ned and my mother almost waltz into the motel
with the food. Sometimes when they are together,
they look so happy to be in each other's company
that they appear in the simplest movements to be
dancing.

After we have eaten and Ned has offered to take us
all to the casino for the umpteenth time and my
mother has looked at the yawning boys and said
no, she is tired too, actually, Ned and I set off.

Ned is looking less nervous now that he has
eaten and showered and it has cooled down outside. He is actually looking pretty sprightly and
energized.

The casino, it turns out, isn't really a theater
where John performs. It is just a big room with a

lot of tables and people drinking. There is a sort of makeshift stage and lighting and, suspended over the stage, a big hanging moon. It is the first thing you notice. It is enormous and obviously made from a blown-up photograph and shows all the craters. You can see the outline of a door in it too, even though I don't think you are supposed to.

Ned has the bag of money in the trunk of the car but he doesn't want to bring it in. We try to go backstage to see his brother but the guy running the lights says we aren't allowed and John isn't there yet anyway.

"But it's seven-thirty," says Ned.

"So?" says the guy.

We return to our little table. Everyone else in the room is drinking away and no one seems the least interested in when the show is starting. There are even two slot machines with people standing around them.

"How are we going to contact him now?" I ask.

"I don't know," Ned says. "Maybe I'll just have to stand up during the show and shout hello or something."

I can't tell if he is kidding. I hope so. That would be so embarrassing.

We sit and drink our Diet Cokes and tap our
toes and finally lights go up on the stage and a
woman in a very sparkling blue costume comes
out to practically no applause. But Ned and I applaud dutifully. She makes some remark about how
John the Amazing is going to be here any minute.
He is just whizzing around the galaxy. "Wait," she
says, "can that be him?" She suddenly rises in the
air. I think it is supposed to look magical but you
can clearly see the harness. Then she floats or
rather is yanked to the giant moon and opens the
door in it and inside is . . . nobody.

"Aw, crap," she says.

Hot on the Trail

"Hal, drop me down!" the woman calls to someone backstage.

"I tole you a hunred times, check to see he's arrived before you start!" yells Hal. "Save yourself a ride." And you can hear him guffawing loudly. He alone seems to be having a delightful time.

She dangles there a bit longer and I am thinking that Hal isn't a very nice guy when suddenly she drops, landing with a thunk on her rear on the stage.

"Hey, WATCH IT!" she yells belatedly into the wings and then a man in a suit comes onstage and says, "Show's over." Just that. No apology. No explanation. He leaves without even helping her up.

"I guess they don't apologize because they know the show is free anyway," I say to Ned.

"Free, ha!" he says. "These Cokes are costing me ten bucks."

"And look, no one is even listening. They're not even moving. They just sit there drinking. No wonder he doesn't bother showing up half the time."

"Come on, let's get out of here," says Ned. "I've got an idea."

We go outside and he leads me around the casino until we are in back of where the stage is. There is another parking lot with a few cars and a back door to the casino.

We start to go in but the girl in the sparkling blue outfit comes out. She hasn't even changed. She's with a man but Ned pulls her aside anyway.

"Listen, you gotta help me," he says. "I'm looking for John. I'm his brother."

"Oh yeah," she says, squinting at Ned's face. "You know, I can sorta see a resemblance."

"No one will tell me where he is."

"Well, jeez, no one knows," she says. "You know, I think he might be gone for good this time. I gotta get a new job 'cause that rat dog isn't coming back. Sorry, I guess no one wants to hear their brother called a rat dog."

"Never mind that," says Ned, waving his hand airily as if calling someone a rat dog is of no consequence and in fact is encouraged in some cultures. "What makes you think he's gone for good?"

"'Cause last night after the show he says to me, 'Shirley, this time I'm going to disappear for good.' I guess I thought he meant the trick. Or something." She frowns, puzzling. "To tell you the truth, I'm not sure what I thought."

I think this may be Shirley's major problem but I don't offer this insight.

"But now, with this new evidence, I think, I mean, like, I can see a different meaning, if you get my take. Like, he meant, like, he was going to take a powder. You think?"

"I don't know," says Ned. "What do you think?"

"Well, gosh, maybe," says the woman in a wondering tone as if no one had ever asked her for an opinion before and it is a momentous occasion. "'Cause I think he's in a bit of trouble."

"Oh no," says Ned.

"Don't worry, he's always in a bit of trouble."

"Any idea where he'd go?" asks Ned.

The woman gets some lines between her eyes as she puzzles this out. This is a very big night for her. Twice someone has wanted to know what she thinks. She is clearly racking her brain for any and all help it can give her.

"Well, gee, he said to never tell no one but his mother lives up somewhere by Elko and sometimes he takes off there. She's got a horse ranch."

"Mom has a *horse* ranch? In *Nevada?*" says Ned. "I don't believe it."

"Oh yeah. I been there. Near Elko," she says again helpfully. Then she stops and she gets those funny lines over her nose again as she has another lightning-quick flash of genius. "Oh yeah, she would be *your* mom too."

"And you say John goes there?"

"On account of you're brothers." She circles back to this in case Ned is having a hard time keeping up with her deductive reasoning.

"Yeah, I know," says Ned. "Now, you say that John goes to my mother's *horse ranch?*"

"Near Elko. Well, I only know he went the one time, 'cause he took me there. He couldn't help it, we were between shows and he thought it would be a good place to hide."

"To *hide*?"

"Oh sure. I used to hide all the time with Johnny."

"He calls himself *Johnny*?"

"No, *I* call him Johnny," says Shirley gently as if Ned is stupid. "'Cause he don't mostly call himself. Anyhow, maybe he's there but don't tell no one I told you. It's, like, his . . ." She pauses. She is at a loss.

"Refuge?" says Ned.

"Yeah. Like with elephants," she says.

"My mother is keeping horses *and elephants*?" squeals Ned.

I nudge Ned in the ribs. "I think she means refuge. There are wildlife refuges with elephants."

The woman nods compassionately at Ned. She knows what it's like to get all mixed up. "Yeah. I always wanted to go to Africa to those elephant refuges. Maybe I'll do that now. You think it costs a lot?"

"Yeah, probably," says Ned, so concentrated on our little problem that he isn't worrying about raining on her parade.

"But, anyhow, if you see him tell him, like, I quit. You know, I don't get paid when he don't show up and he hasn't been showing up regular lately. Okay? Like, how am I ever going to get to see elephants?"

"Yeah, sure. And listen, don't tell anyone else about the horse ranch," says Ned.

"Hey, I told *you*," says Shirley in outraged tones. "It was, like, *my* secret. Maybe you shouldn't tell anyone about *the elephants*."

"Right," says Ned. "Listen, do you know exactly where this ranch is?"

"Near *Elko*," says Shirley, enunciating as if he is deaf.

"Can you be more specific?"

"You mean like an address or something?" says Shirley, looking confused.

"Yeah, like an address," says Ned.

"Nah, I don't pay attention to things like that," says Shirley. "I'm kind of an in-the-moment girl."

"I can see that," says Ned.

"So where's the guy I come out with?" asks Shirley, looking around the parking lot, but he has disappeared too. "Oh jeez, when it rains it pours." She gets into a beaten-up old black car and speeds away with rubber burning.

We walk back to the car.

"She's not the brightest lightbulb in the box," I say to Ned. "I mean, she had no proof you were John's brother. For all she knew you were one of the guys showing up to give John trouble. But she went ahead and told you where to find him."

"I know," says Ned, ruffling his hair in weariness. It stands up on end as if it has been gelled, but it's just sweat. "We're lucky anyhow that she was a trusting soul, because no one else around here seems to be."

"Maybe it's all this gambling," I say. "Everyone looks kind of lean and desperate. So maybe they prey on each other and after a while no one really trusts anyone else."

"You could say that about an awful lot of places, Bibles," says Ned.

"Whoa!" I say.

"I've been around, Bibles, I've been around," he says, but jovially, and smoothes his hair back down. Now it is lying as if gelled flat. He's really not having a good hair day.

"What kind of trouble do you think John is in?" I ask as we get back in our car.

"Well, if it's the kind that comes accessorized with a bag full of money, I don't even want to guess," says Ned.

We drive silently back to the motel. The bright lights keep flashing even though we are far away from the Strip. I am suddenly tired of all the speed and noise and light here and I just want to sit quietly on our porch in Massachusetts and listen to the waves.

After we park, Ned and I go to our motel rooms, but no one is in mine. I go into the other one, where everyone is awake and dressed. My mother is sitting ramrod straight on the bed, looking unusually prim, her knees together, her hands folded in her lap as if she is waiting for a bus.

"What's the matter?" I ask when I see their stricken faces.

"Bedbugs," says Ned, looking defeated.

"It's DISGUSTING!" yells Maya.

"We'll have to find another motel," says my mother. "We can't sleep here."

"I've got a better idea," says Ned, suddenly brightening. "Who wants to go to Elko?"

· · · · · · · · · · ·

We collect our things and head out into the night. Then we start driving north.

"Where are we going *now*?" asks Maya.

"We're going to visit my mother," says Ned. "She has a horse ranch up in cowboy country."

"Cool," says Max.

"Cool," says Hershel.

"I can't believe I am finally going to meet your mother," says my mother.

"Yeah," says Ned unenthusiastically.

"Where's your mother been?" asks Maya.

"Well, that *is* the question," says Ned. "Not that I was looking real hard."

"Ned . . . ," says my mother.

"All right, aterlay," says Ned.

"That's 'later' in Pig Latin," says Maya.

"Who taught you Pig Latin?" asks Ned. "Not Mrs. Gunderson?"

"Mrs. Gunderson speaks five languages," says Maya enigmatically.

"There's the moon!" screams Hershel, pointing out the window.

Tonight it is a luminous cream-colored orb. Why does the moon always look different? Always different, always personal.

"Listen, you kids may as well go to sleep. It's a long, long drive ahead of us."

"How are you going to find your mom's ranch?" I ask.

"I'll stop in at the sheriff's. Sheriffs at these sparsely populated places know everyone. Especially the ranch owners. I think."

"Jane, can you get some blankets out of the box by your feet? Max and Hershel, why don't you take a blanket and curl up?" says my mother.

I pass out blankets to all. Ned has the heater on but it doesn't work very well. The car was old when Ned bought it two years ago and things keep going wrong that we can't afford to fix. I like being a little chilly with a blanket wrapped around me like a tent. It is also a place to escape from Maya. My mother wears a blanket as well. Only Ned has to be blanketless and cold but he says he doesn't mind. He seems distracted and angry when we mention his mother. Angry is a new mode to observe him in. In the past two years I have barely ever seen him so.

All is quiet in the car. Maya falls asleep quickly. I had expected more pressing questions from her, her voice had that tone, but I guess she is too tired. Max and Hershel are completely worn out. I would like to sleep but I know that my mother and Ned are just waiting for us all to drift off so they can discuss this new turn of events. I pretend to doze. I let my head roll from side to side in case they are sneaking peeks at me through the rearview mirror. Then I start to breathe deeply and rhythmically. This is harder than you'd think. Finally, when they still do not speak, I begin to give out a little snore now and then. I hope I am not overdoing it. I am almost asleep for real when my mother says in a quiet voice, "So, what happens next?"

"We see if he's at my mother's ranch. If he is we give him the money."

"What if he isn't?"

"I don't know. Maybe leave it in the desert and go back to Massachusetts. The whole thing has the feel of a wild-goose chase. I'll tell you one thing, if she knows he's in trouble, I'd be surprised if she takes him in. Self-sacrifice and maternal protectiveness have never been her strong suits."

"No, you always describe her as if, after your father left, she wasn't quite there," says my mother.

Ned snorts. "No, she was thereabouts."

I stare out the back window at the stars. The whole back of the station wagon window shows a sky resplendent with constellations. The universe goes out forever. Night covers the desert like a blanket. There is nothing like a sky full of stars to make you lose track of your thoughts. For instance, at first, you realize that all those stars, all those pinpricks of light, are far away from each other but repeated all over the sky thousands of times. They are each glowing hugely alone but not, connected by the deep dark of the universe, part of a whole picture of what we see, the night sky. The same and all different. Not aware of the picture they present as a whole. But not seeing us below either, the vastness of each of us and the many. Not, for instance, understanding that all these dots below are divided, into such things as Democratic and Republican parties. People who like sweet things and people who like salty or sour. People who put FREE TIBET bumper stickers on their cars and people who put THE MORE PEOPLE I MEET THE MORE I LOVE MY DOG and things like that on their bumpers. Actually, people who put anything at all on their bumpers and people who don't. Then I just gaze contentedly at the stars and don't bother trying to think about anything.

But later it occurs to me how Ned and I wanted to be outlaws and here we are, in the American West, in the high desert. We are escaping who knows what with a bunch of money from who knows where. Do things happen because you want them to? Can you create your life and adventures by imagining them? My head lolls from side to side for real now and when I next wake up, it is morning.

I open my eyes and stretch. I have woken up because instead of the smooth gliding asphalt beneath the wheels, we are bumping along over potholes and spitting gravel. Then I see it is not so much a road as a long driveway. Land stretches in all directions but there is a barbed-wire fence. The fence with its leaning old wood posts serves only to accentuate the vast emptiness of the land. The fence slants in disarray and there is a rightness to this too. This is not a country that values uprightness. In the distance is an old-fashioned windmill. The kind you see from time to time on the plains or the desert, looking as if they have been left here by time in a place that doesn't change from century to century. They stand in the windswept dust and turn for no one but they still turn.

"Where are we?" I ask.

"At Ned's mother's ranch," says my mother, yawning.

"How did we find it?" I ask.

"We stopped in town about half an hour ago and got directions. You were asleep," says Ned.

We pull up in front of a big falling-down house.

All the paint has been chipped off the siding by the centuries. When you look at it you see the decades that have gone by. A woman rushes out onto the porch. She squints her eyes to see who it is and yells, "NED!"

Dorothy's Invitation

The woman flings herself at the car and practically drags him out of it. This reminds me of my mother's first meeting with Ned on the beach when she ran across the sand and flung herself on him. If you want people yelling your name and flinging themselves on you, all you have to do is disappear for years at a time. It doesn't seem fair somehow. Shouldn't they upbraid him a little first for his neglect?

"Hi, Mom," says Ned.

"Look at you. What are you doing here?"

Ned, who has been hugging her, drops his arms and steps back. "Actually, I'm looking for John."

"Well, lordy Maudey, what do you want with *him*?"

"I've got something that I believe belongs to him."

"Money," says Ned's mother, sighing; then she turns abruptly and walks to the porch and starts up the steps. We follow her. "I can't say I'm surprised. How do you think I got this ranch? John bought it. It rightly belongs to him. There's more of his money in it than mine. Where he got the money, I don't know."

"You bought a *ranch* with John's money?" says Ned.

His mother stops and turns around and gives him a level stare, which because she is one step higher than him brings them eye to eye. "Well, not entirely with his money. I did have some of my own. Your father, when he died, left me some. *That* was a surprise."

"Dad died?"

"You haven't exactly been in touch, have you?"

"Wow, Dad died," says Ned, and sits down right there on the steps.

"Well, John doesn't think so. He thinks that your

father just decided to disappear on a more permanent basis. He thinks he's in Alaska somewhere and didn't want to leave a trail so he faked his own death."

"Oh, come on!"

"Well, there wasn't a body, Neddie. He left a suicide note saying he was going to drown himself in the Fraser River and even though they never found his body the police said they had no reason to doubt him so they probated his estate—is that the word I want?—and I got it all and so I wasn't going to argue."

"Oh jeez, why disappear? He was never in contact with anyone anyway."

"'Cause that's what people in this family like to do, Ned. Look at you. Look at John. It's in the blood. Anyhow, John said there was some talk that your dad had a new girlfriend and they staged the disappearance for her sake or something. Said they're off together in Alaska having a nice ripping old time of it. Hope they freeze their butts off."

"Mom," says Ned.

"So there are kids with you," says Ned's mom,

looking down for the first time at the four of us. We all have sleep creases on our faces and the boys are wrapped in their blankets. She sighs again. "All right, come in, the lot of you. I'll make breakfast. Take your shoes off outside."

"Mom, what's with the horses?" asks Ned.

"Like I said, Ned, you haven't been in touch," says his mother, and disappears inside.

We follow her into the house. In the kitchen we all stand around awkwardly while she goes to the fridge and gets out eggs and bacon. She puts an apron on and silently begins the production of food for seven people. "I don't know, Neddie, I don't know what to think about you showing up like this twenty-some years later. When I saw you last you were a boy. Now you look so old."

"Gee, thanks, Mom," says Ned.

"I'm Felicity," says my mother. It's been hard to know where to jump in through this whole conversation.

"Well, good for you," says Ned's mother. "I'm Dorothy."

"I'm Ned's wife," says my mother.

"OH LORDY!" says Dorothy, and leaves the skillet where she has been turning bacon. Her apron is already scatter-shot with grease but she throws her arms around my mother anyway. "Why didn't you say so in the first place? Forgive me, dear. I thought you were just another one of the boys' women. Seems like they're always bringing them around like lost animals. Last one John brought around wore sequins and I could see she was going to come to no good end. So all these children are yours and Neddie's? So I'm a grand-mother?"

"I had all these children already when Ned married me," says my mother. "Of course, you can be their grandmother if you like."

I notice that this doesn't really answer the question of whether Ned has fathered any of us. But I suppose now would not be the time for my mother to start revealing bloodlines.

"Well, thank you, I believe I'll take you up on that. Four instantaneous grandkids. And I don't care what happens to you and Neddie. If you divorce. If you separate. If one of you gets yourself shot or jailed. Don't matter. These grandkids are going to be mine forever. That's that." She claps her hands together for emphasis.

Her zeal is a little frightening. We all take a step back but she doesn't seem to notice.

"Now, this is worth celebrating. Never mind eggs, let's have PANCAKES!"

"Yay!" says Hershel.

"Yay!" says Max.

"Want to see the Viking bone?" asks Hershel. I think the idea of celebrating with cake, even pancakes, reminds him of the first time Ned brought out the Viking bone. When we were having cupcakes on the beach in Massachusetts.

"Maybe later, dear," says Ned's mom. "Now, I want you all to call me Dorothy, okay? You can even call me Grandma Dorothy."

"Nobody had children?" asks Ned.

"Not a one," says Dorothy.

"Not even the girls?"

"Feh." Dorothy spits in the direction of the sink. "I don't know where things went wrong with this family but no one seems to have the slightest interest in procreating. Okay, boys, you can take turns stirring this batter. And you"—

she points at me—"what did you say your name was?"

"Jane," I say.

"Good name. Like a plain name. And the other one?" She points at Maya, who pulls her blanket closer so it is almost over her face.

"Maya," I say.

"Yeah, you two reach up on those shelves and set the table. Now that we're family we can all pitch in. Isn't this cozy?"

My mother has already grabbed a spare apron off a nail by the stove and is turning bacon and scrambling eggs. Soon we have everything on the table, the enticing smells of fried foods and maple syrup enveloping the warm farm kitchen.

"Now," says Dorothy when we all sit down. "What's this about John?"

"Aterlay, Mom," says Ned.

"That's 'later' in Pig Latin," says Maya to Dorothy.

"Abokabay," says Dorothy.

Maya furrows her brow. "That's not Pig Latin," she says.

"It's Abenglabish," says Dorothy. "You put 'ab' at the beginning of the word and between syllables."

"Well, I don't like it," says Maya.

"Who cares?" says Dorothy. "Have some more pancakes."

Maya frowns at Dorothy even harder. No one has ever talked to Maya this way. Particularly when she has on her fierce face, as she does right now. She doesn't seem to know how to deal with it. The best she can do is glare menacingly and when this has no effect she shrugs and takes more pancakes.

After we eat, everyone helps to clean things up except Max and Hershel, who want to know if they can go out and pet the horses. Dorothy says that is fine but they must get one of the young men out there to go with them. She says there's Ben and Leeron and Hank.

"You girls want to go too?" asks Dorothy.

"I don't like horses," says Maya, although as far as I know she has never been around one before. "Do you have a television?"

"Up in my bedroom," says Dorothy.

"MAYA!" I say. "At ten o'clock in the *morning*?"

But Maya runs upstairs.

"Okay, Mom," says Ned. "I got a duffel bag of

money in the car. John left it up with the Carriers in B.C. If I leave it with you, you can give it to him next time you see him."

"I wouldn't count on it. I expect I've seen the last of him for a while, now that I won't let him launder his money here anymore. I said I'd take his money once but no more."

"Do you know for sure he was laundering it?" asks Ned.

"What do you mean laundering the money?" I ask him.

"It means that John sort of hides the illegal way he got the money by giving it to my mother to buy a ranch. People lose track of the money and then when my mother sells the ranch, if she does, she can just give John a gift of the money and no one suspects it was his in the first place."

"That's confusing," I say.

"It's meant to be," says Ned. "That's how people hide money—by confusing everyone."

"Well, how did he get it illegally to begin with?" I ask.

"I don't know. Do you know, Mom?" asks Ned.

"Gosh no," says Dorothy. "I don't even know for sure that it is illegal. John says it isn't. He says he won it gambling."

"But you don't believe him?" asks Ned.

"If he won it gambling, why not just put it in the bank?" asks Dorothy.

"Exactly," says Ned. "Which is why I went to Las Vegas to give it back to him. I don't want a bag of illegal money."

"Well, I was willing to give John and his money the benefit of the doubt the first time. People do win big sometimes. But if he's dropping bags of the stuff in the woods, then I think we gotta think the worst. So how'd you find me if you couldn't find John?"

"I ran into his magic assistant," says Ned.

"Oh, Miss Sequins," says Dorothy.

"Right. She told me."

"I'm surprised she remembered. She didn't strike me as real smart."

"Well, no," says Ned.

"Anyhow, let's talk of happier things. So, I take it you'll be spending the summer here," says Dorothy. "Let me get to know my grandchildren."

"When have you ever been interested in children?" asks Ned, gnawing on some bacon.

"We're family," says Dorothy.

"You don't even know where any of us live."

"Well, you boys may make a point of disappearing but I'll have you know I get Christmas cards regular from the girls. I don't know why you say such things."

"You didn't know our whereabouts when we were growing up," says Ned.

"I did too!" says Dorothy.

"Nelda took off for six weeks once when she was thirteen and you didn't do anything about it until the social worker came by."

"Well, you can't keep track of everyone all the time, Neddie."

"And Maureen took the bus all the way to the Maritimes the summer she was fifteen and you didn't even ask her what she wanted to do there."

"I assumed she wanted to see the Maritimes!"

"Didn't it occur to you it was a little dangerous, a girl that age traveling alone with hardly any money?"

"Well, life's a dangerous business, Neddie. I expect you know that by now. You can't really keep anyone safe. So how about it? Stay here. I bet the boys would love a summer on a real horse ranch."

"Naw, we're heading back to Massachusetts, Mom," says Ned. "Maybe we'll spend a day or two to rest up. I don't know what to do about the money."

"Well, me either," says Dorothy. "How about we take it to the sheriff and tell him we found it by the side of the road?"

"They'd still want to know where we got it. Then they'd start investigating us. I think it's asking for trouble. Besides, suppose, and I know this is unlikely, but just *suppose* we're wrong and John earned it legitimately? What if he's become one of those people who don't trust banks and want to hide their money in their mattress or something?"

"I'll tell you what I think about that," says Dorothy. "People who got their money legit want to hide it in their mattresses. People who didn't get their money legit want to hide it in other people's mattresses. What I think I got here, in this ranch, is a mattress full of someone else's money."

We all go out and sit on the porch and rock in rocking chairs and on the porch swing.

"Well, we've got a little time to think about how to handle the money," says my mother.

"Sure you do," says Dorothy. "Look at that red-tailed hawk, Felicity. My, my. I do like the red-tailed hawks. You got as much time as you want. Stay and work on that novel, Ned."

"What novel?" asks Ned, his eyes working back and forth. He is starting to pick up the pace of his rocking.

"That novel you said you were always going to write," says Dorothy. She's rocking slow and easy now with a little smug smile on her face.

"That was years ago," says Ned, really working the rocker now.

"Ned writes pieces for CBC. That's the Canadian Broadcasting Corporation. He writes essays about all kinds of things, and travelogues," I pipe up.

"Really? People pay for that?" asks Dorothy.

"Yes," says Ned.

"Well, wouldn't you like to do some real writing

instead of that fluff?" asks Dorothy. "And now you can. It's lonely here on the ranch, you know, with just Ben and the boys coming to help out. Nothing but a lot of tumbleweed."

"So move into town," says Ned. His rocker slows down, hers speeds up.

"I like horses," says Dorothy. "I'm staying put. Easier for you all just to stay here."

Ned starts rocking more quickly. "I already said we can't."

"I didn't hear from Felicity," says Dorothy. But she doesn't turn to my mother, she's still looking at Ned.

"It's Felicity's house we're going back to," says Ned. "Of course she wants to go home. Nobody in their right mind would want to stay in Nevada."

Dorothy rocks faster. Ned slows down. Then Dorothy slows down a little.

"Foolish," she says. "Well, if I can't convince you, I can't. No one could ever convince you to do anything you didn't intend to do in the first place. So, come on, Jane. I'm going out to ride Satan and you can watch."

Frankly, I'm surprised she gave in so quickly;

things seemed to be building to a great explosive logjam and then, pffff, nothing.

"Sure," I say politely.

"Ben!" she calls in the direction of the stable. "Saddle up Satan, I'm going to show Jane how to ride."

"You don't want to do that, Mrs. N!" calls a voice. A young man emerges from the barn. He's short and muscular and lithe. "He's in a mood today."

"I don't care," she says. "I'll knock some sense into him. Come on, Jane, gotta get my riding boots on, they're in the tack room."

"I never envisioned your mother as a cowgirl," says my mother to Ned as we leave the porch.

"A real Annie Oakley. You know she's got a shotgun in the china cupboard? I saw it when I put the platter away."

"Not loaded, I hope," says my mother.

"Don't worry, Felicity," calls Dorothy over her shoulder. "I keep the shells up top of the cupboard where kids can't reach, and the shotgun's never loaded. But I like knowing it's there."

I follow her into the tack room and she changes

into riding boots. "Satan was my first horse. I knew nothing about buying horses in those days and just got him because he's a magnificent-looking beast. But he's a stallion and he's mean. I should've known better than to buy a male. Never had any luck with males. Ben thinks I should set him free. He says horses like that ought never to be kept."

"Huh," I say, because I have no idea really what she is talking about. She seems full of opinions, not the way I pictured her when Ned described how she was kind of vacant after his dad left. I thought she was going to be one of those hollow long-suffering women with dark haunted eyes and a victimish manner. Instead she seems perfectly capable of taking care of herself and getting what she wants.

We go to the riding ring, where Ben is holding the reins of a huge black snorting beast.

"You see what I mean?" asks Dorothy, mounting him. "You stay outside the ring, Jane. You too, Ben. He's meaner than a snake today."

"You oughtn't be on him," says Ben, and he goes back to the barn. I turn to see Max and Hershel happily carrying forkfuls of horse manure and putting it in a wheelbarrow. I wonder if they know what it is. They probably do. It would be like them to enjoy nothing more than messing around with a manure pile. Hershel has some smeared on one cheek.

I hear a scream and turn my head to see that Dorothy has been thrown from Satan and has landed on her back.

Ben comes flying out of the barn, vaults the ring and grabs Satan's reins, pulling him away to keep him from running over Dorothy. My mother yells, "Call 911," and then, in a flutter, seems to realize that there is no one but Maya in the house and so runs into the house to do it herself. I start to go into the ring to help Dorothy but Ben yells, "Don't touch her! If she broke her back she needs to stay still."

"I don't think it's my darned back, I think I broke my hip," moans Dorothy, but at least she is talking.

The ambulance is faster than you would think so far out in the country.

The paramedics put Dorothy on a backboard

and onto a gurney. All through this I should be horrified but instead I cannot get out of my head the sight of Ben, as if he doesn't have to deal with gravity the way the rest of us do, flying out of the barn and in one fluid motion vaulting the ring and grabbing Satan's reins. There is grace here and courage and intelligence and something else, an ability to see what needs to be done in a flash and do it.

I keep replaying the scene in my head, only in my fantasy it is me on the ground and he picks me up and carries me out of the ring. Then I imagine we are in the wild flat plains and he is rescuing me from a whole herd of wild mustangs. They really do have wild mustangs in Nevada so this is not that far a stretch. Me and Ben and the mustangs. His hair flying back as his one hand projects him over the top rail.

"Ned, go ahead with her to the hospital and I'll stay here with the children," says my mother as they follow the paramedics to the ambulance. Suddenly their marriage seems dull and prosaic. How could I ever have thought they were having a romance? What do they know of romance?

I trail slightly behind them unthinkingly because I don't know what else to do and it is because of this I hear my mother say to Ned, "Your poor mother!" and Ned whisper back, "Yeah, right. We can't go now. Look who got the last word."

Ned's Sisters

We are sitting in Dorothy's bedroom, where Maya has taken to hanging out about eight hours a day, watching game shows and soap operas, talk shows and the occasional news broadcast. I come in sometimes to hear Dorothy saying things like "Maya, let's take a break from *The Price Is Right* and see what is happening in the world." She has just said this and Maya has nodded and the two of them are sitting spellbound through floods and fires and abductions and philandering politicians and Maya puts the knuckles of her right hand to the side of her mouth, a gesture she has taken to making more and more often and which looks perilously close to thumb-sucking to me. Then, having fulfilled their current-events duty, they switch solemnly back to a screen full of shrieking contestants and horrible music and ugly colored lights and sets. I don't know which is worse. But at least during the game shows, Maya's hand moves away from her mouth.

Ned has taken the boys into town to buy grain and my mother is busy scouting all over for Ned's sisters' phone numbers. Dorothy claimed to have written them down somewhere but then couldn't remember where she put the paper so she asked my mother to comb through drawers. The first drawer my mother opened was in the buffet and it was crammed so tightly with string and old glasses and photographs and random pieces of paper that the drawer practically popped out, spilling its contents everywhere.

"This may take a while," said my mother, so I've gone upstairs to see what Maya is up to. I cannot watch *The Price Is Right* and am hoping to talk Maya into playing a game of cards when we hear the wolves. It is a long harmonious song of many voices. It is so startling that it makes Dorothy click off the TV, which is something of a miracle. The miracle of the wolves, I think. Or perhaps the miracle of the channel changer. But it turns out to be a miracle in more ways than one because Dorothy says, "There are no wolves in Nevada!"

"There are no wolves, period," agrees Maya hopefully.

"That sure sounded like wolves to me," I say. "We heard them up in northern B.C. and they sounded just like that."

"But there are no wolves in Nevada," says Dorothy. "Haven't been for years. Anyhow, Maya, you're safe as long as you stay in this room, just like I'm safe as long as I'm in this house. This is my safe place. They're going to have to take me out of here feetfirst, toes up, in a coffin. You got it? You know why it's so safe here? Because it's the first house I found where you can look out any window and see the horizon in any direction. You can always see what's coming before it gets you. And horses will warn you too. They're like dogs in that respect. Now, you look out that window and I bet you don't see any wolves. Let's see what else is on TV."

I think this is pretty creepy and a terrible thing to tell Maya. But I don't know how to undo it without being rude.

Dorothy holds out the clicker and presses the On button. Wolf-wonder can only interest her for so long. There are large all-terrain vehicles to be won and hair products to price. It's funny what some people think is real and choose to give their attention to. Those hair products and big refrigerators seem far more unreal to me than the wolves. Maya's knuckles return firmly to her cheek but her face relaxes as she is drawn into the excitement of a woman trying to win a set of golf clubs.

At dinner my mother tells Ned that she has called all three of his sisters.

"My sisters?" he squawks, putting down his fork. "Maureen?"

My mother nods, chewing a mouthful of mashed potatoes. My mother makes the best mashed potatoes in the world. She adds a lot of chopped fresh parsley. I could eat an entire dinner of nothing but her potatoes.

"Nelda?"

My mother swallows and nods.

"Candace?"

"Yes, she seemed kind of strange," says my mother.

"Strange how?"

"Well, it's hard to say. It was a difficult phone call for her, after all, hearing that her mother broke her hip and fractured some vertebrae and will never walk without a walker again. Being asked to come see her after so many years. It seemed a little odd to all your sisters, I'm sure. And they didn't know who I was. But Candace seemed, I don't know, she kept making me repeat everything and then when I asked if we had a bad connection, she said no, she was just texting various people on her BlackBerry and after that she kept putting me on hold so she could take other calls."

"What does she do?" asks Ned.

"She's a realtor."

"Oh well, that explains it. They're all like that. Totally insane."

"Really?" says my mother. "I suppose nowadays they all have cell phones glued to their ears. It wasn't quite so bad when I dealt with them."

"When were you dealing with realtors?"

"Oh, you know, after I inherited the beach house. They all wanted me to sell it."

"Oh yes, the beach house," says Ned, chewing away. "Good potatoes."

"What about the beach house?" I ask.

"Back when I got it, well, I guess a few years after that, actually, beach property got to be more in
demand and so realtors were always calling, fish-
ing around, hoping I'd sell. A lot of them got sand
in their good shoes walking over the beach and
knocking on my door."

"See what I mean? They're desperate people,"
says Ned through another mouthful of potatoes. A
glob drops from the edge of his mouth onto his
plate, like snow falling off the roof, and the boys
laugh.

"Did you ever want to sell?" I ask. There is nothing like finding out things you have never known
about members of your own family.

"No, of course not. Never," says my mother.
"What could I buy with the money that I would
want more?"

"Nothing," I say.

"Right," says Ned, who is conflicted because he
is trying to eat potatoes and get information all at
the same time. It is always a hard choice when it's
my mother's mashed potatoes. The first instinct is
to remain silent so as to be able to consume more

rapidly. "Well, gosh, how did you even know where to find my sisters?"

"The Christmas cards," says my mother.

"Oh, right, the Christmas cards," says Ned dismissively.

"Dorothy told me that your sisters had each enclosed her phone number with her card. Dorothy was annoyed because they enclosed their phone numbers instead of just picking up a phone and calling her, so she never called them either. But she squirreled the cards away somewhere and couldn't remember where. It took me most of the morning to find them," says my mother.

"There, you see!" says Ned as if this explains it all.

"I see," says Hershel.

"I see too," says Max.

They are unwavering in their support.

"You see *what*?" asks Maya.

I frown. I take this as a sign that all this TV watching with Dorothy has put Maya firmly on her side, if sides must be chosen.

"Anyhow, the upshot is that they are all coming for a nice little visit," says my mother.

"They're coming for a *visit?*" says Ned, and he drops his fork into his lap. I laugh.

"Well, yes, I invited them. I mean, something has to be done about your mother when we go back to Massachusetts. I thought they might want to come and visit too. Dorothy won't walk properly again. Someone has to tell her and someone has to help her figure out what's next."

Ned's mouth works for a few minutes and no sounds come out and then finally he says, "Jeepers."

"Jeepers," says Max.

"Jeepers," says Hershel.

"What's for dessert?" asks Maya.

The next problem is where to put everyone. My mother and Ned have one of the farmhouse's big bedrooms. Maya and I have another and the boys another and Dorothy has her own. Finally it is decided that a cot can go into Dorothy's room for Maya, since they have become so simpatico, and an extra cot can be moved into our twin-bedded bedroom so that the three sisters can all sleep there, and I can sleep in the pantry.

"In the pantry?" I say plaintively to Ned as he helps me move out all the cans and jars to make room. "With the *rats?*"

"Oh, come on, Bibles, there aren't any rats. Besides, don't blame me, blame your mother, this whole thing was her idea."

"Well, you did say we were leaving for Massachusetts so that means someone has to be here to care for Dorothy," I say.

"I know, I know," mutters Ned. He is nervous. How can someone's family make him so nervous?

The first one to arrive is Maureen. She is fat and a lot older than Ned, I think. She looks to be at least fifty and her face hangs in pleasant jowls. She has a farm in Ontario that she shared with her husband for years before he died of a heart attack. She shows us a picture of the two of them standing on their front porch together. He is hugely fat and jolly-looking. I think running her farm alone, the lone fat soul on all those acres of corn, must be very sad for her.

The second one is Nelda and she is as thin as Maureen is fat. Her hair is dyed black and she wrings her hands a lot. She looks sort of like a bird and she wears a big bejeweled uncomfortable-looking cross around her neck. Maureen tells me privately that Nelda has become a Catholic and no one has trusted her since. "She sends *religious* Christmas cards," she says to me.

I like Maureen because she talks to me like I am an adult and because that first night when we are all together, after supper when we are sitting on the porch watching Ben work the horses, she says, "Look at that young man. If I were a girl, I'd make a play for him. Ah, me, to be that age again!"

"Sex on a stick," says Candace, the realtor sister. She has just arrived this evening, during supper, actually, and no one knows what to make of her. She has a very young modern haircut and her hair is dyed blond. She has lots of wrinkles around her eyes and mouth and she dresses in clothes that aren't too tight exactly but are maybe a little tight for how old she is. She clicks her nails on the table a lot and without moving much always gives the appearance of a lot of restless decisive motion that nonetheless achieves nothing. It is as if she is try-ing to hatch an egg.

Ned and my mother are in the kitchen dishing

up dessert so they don't hear this remark about sex on a stick, but Maureen and Nelda do. They glance over at Candace and give her a funny look.

Dorothy can't come down the stairs and Maya is having her dessert upstairs with her. The boys are racing around the barnyard. They are perpetual-motion machines or like the law of inertia. When they are running around nothing stops them unless we pin them down and then you put some food into them and they are asleep and they sleep the sleep of the dead until the movement begins again. Boys are so uncomplicated, I think. They move, they eat, they sleep; they don't spend endless amounts of time thinking about it all like girls. They pretty much do this until they wear themselves out and die.

Right now I see Satan going round and round the ring. His eye occasionally meets mine. There is something deep and eternal there. It is time itself in the horse's eye.

Hershel and Max have made friends with Hank and Leeron, the other ranch hands, who are older than Ben and seem to really like the boys. Ben tends to ignore them. I think he is only interested in the horses.

I am watching Ben working a horse now and wondering how old he is. I tried to find this out by casually asking Dorothy if Ben was going to college but instead of giving me an indication of his age she just said, "Oh, he doesn't care about college. He just wants to own a ranch."

There was no way to find out anything after that without being too obvious.

Ned and my mom come out with trays of pie and hand it out to all of us.

"So," says Ned, sitting down on the steps.

"Why are steps so much more fun to sit on than chairs?" I ask Ned.

"I don't know, Bibles," says Ned, stretching his long legs. "So, nice to see you all." He points his fork at his sisters.

"It's a surprise, I'll give you that," says Maureen, inhaling her pie.

"It's a blessing," says Nelda in her mousy little voice, and I can just feel Ned rolling his eyes.

"The first thing to do," says Candace, attacking her pie with businesslike decisiveness and a lot of extra unnecessary movements, "is to get her to sell those horses."

"I know," says Ned.

"But she *loves* those horses," I say.

"Loves them, schmoves them," says Candace. "They're a drain on her resources. Financial and everything else. And now they're just plain impractical. She'll never ride again. She'll never even walk well again with the spinal injury. And she ought to move into town, where she can get around on one of those scooters. That would at least give her a little mobility."

"Oh yes, a scooter," says Maureen, getting up for a second piece of pie. "Anyone else want one?" she calls over her shoulder on her way into the kitchen.

"And she's all isolated out here," says Nelda in her whispery little voice. "*Anything* could happen."

"Exactly. She told me she heard wolves the other day," says Maureen, coming back onto the porch and snorting.

"She did," I say. "We all did. That is, she and Maya and I."

"I heard them too," says my mother. "Calling over the desert."

"Well, that's it, then. She can't live with wolves. I mean, honestly," says Candace. "It's good that you called us, Neddie. Enough with the horses and wolves. Whole thing is just plain impractical. It's like the time she moved us all up to Fort McMurray. Remember that? No job. No friends. No nothing."

"Yes," says Maureen, putting down her fork and looking at us all plaintively. "*Why* did she do that? Did you ever wonder?"

"All the time," says Candace.

"It was *weird*"—Nelda stops and looks down into her lap as if she has frightened herself by using such an assertive word—"behavior."

"Well, it wasn't *normal*," says Ned. "It wasn't what normal people do."

"Did you ever *ask* her?" asks my mother.

"Oh, you don't ask people in my family questions like that, honey," says Ned. Since when did he start to call her honey? He is drawing an invisible circle around himself and her with it, setting them apart from his birth family. "It's bad form."

"But you want to know," insists my mother. "You all do."

"She couldn't tell you, anyhow, Felicity, trust us. She's not an introspective sort," says Candace. "And if she could she wouldn't."

"That's right," says Maureen.

"And incidentally, I *did* ask her not long after we moved there. I said, 'What the heck are we doing here?'" says Candace.

"You didn't!" says Maureen. "You never told us that. What did she say?"

"Nothing."

"But that's not really the same question, is it?" persists my mother. "'Why did you do it?' and 'What are we doing here?' are really different questions, aren't they? She might have no more idea than you what you were suddenly doing there even though she knew why she did it." But no one is paying attention to her. I don't think they understand what she is trying to say and they don't know her well enough to know it's worth making the effort.

"It would be like her to say nothing," says Maureen.

"So, so much for asking her," says Candace, sighing.

"Well, anyway, we're agreed about the horses," says Ned.

"Yep," says Candace. "The horses have to go."

"What about the ranch? Think you could sell it, Candace?"

"Oh, probably if I had time to hang around, which I don't, but I'll find a good realtor in town. And I'll do some research and make sure we set a good price. Anyhow, I'm sure she'll see it's for the best since she knows she can't walk properly again. I don't know what her choices are except to hire a round-the-clock nurse and live here and that would cost the earth and wipe out any savings she has and it would come to a move back into town eventually anyway. Might as well do it now."

"Well," says Ned, and he scuffs his shoe around on the porch. "I don't think she really knows about not walking."

"What do you mean?" snaps Candace.

"Well, the doctor thought it would be better if she got that information introduced kind of gentle-like from, um, family. He said it's always a hard pill to swallow."

"And you didn't want to be the one to give her the pill," says Maureen.

"Hey, you can any of you volunteer right now. No reason it has to be me," says Ned.

"Thanks," says Candace. "This is just great. So now we have to tell her she won't walk the same way ever again and she needs to sell the ranch?"

"Looks like," says Ned.

"You do it, Neddie," says Nelda.

"Why me?" asks Ned.

"Because you got here first," says Candace. Nelda and Maureen nod.

"But where will she go?" asks Nelda.

"Why don't you go into town and look for someplace, Nelda? Someplace sort of nice to tempt her," says Candace.

"Have you *seen* the town? It's not exactly a flourishing metropolis. If you can find a home of *any* sort, *pounce* on it, I say," says Maureen. "And after all, she can't be too picky, she's lived in Fort McMurray. She made *us* live in Fort McMurray. It's not like she's been living in Paris all her life. She knows small desperate towns. She should be very comfortable in one."

"All right, that's Nelda's job, then," says Candace. "We ought to split up the arrangements to be made evenly. There's enough to go around. And Ned, you and your family can hang out for the summer until she gets the place sold, right?"

"Now, wait one cotton-pickin' minute," says Ned, and it degenerates into a lot of boring talk about who can and can't do what and they look to be going at it all night so I sneak off the porch.

No one even notices me go and I hang over the ring and watch Ben. I am hoping he will offer to teach me to ride or to come into the ring with him but he doesn't even seem to notice that I am here. Maureen says she would make a play for him but how does she mean she would do this? I can't even get him to look at me. Hi, Ben, I think, trying to send thought waves into his head, Hi, Ben, look at me, Ben.

I like Ned's sisters and I like having them around. They are all so different and it is interesting to have a house full of women. I think it must be nice for my mother as well. She gets along with all of them. But as much as I enjoy this, strategically it might be better if they left so that I could be more visibly helpful. I have visions of myself spending the summer with Dorothy on the porch. I would bring her glasses of iced tea and read to her in a ministering angel way and I would be the one to find a spectacular new living arrangement for her. But, of course, I would be too modest to accept any credit for this, although Ned and my mother and Dorothy would all praise me loudly on the porch where Ben could hear and he would find out what a quiet unassuming but spectacularly saint-like and efficient person I am. It would be the kind of thing he would appreciate. I think he's a stand-up, go-to, quietly-get-things-done kind of guy. I can imagine this is what he would admire in a girl too.

Then over the sound of the horse's hooves thundering round the ring comes the clear call of the wolves. I hear all talk stop on the porch.

"Darn it, someone's going to have to do something about those wolves. Hank, Leeron, let's go check fences!" Ben yells.

Ben puts down the lunge whip and vaults over the ring. He is covered in sweat and dust. He is so close to me I can smell him. But he still doesn't look at me. He disappears into the barn and Hank comes out, attaches the lead to Satan and takes him back to his stall. Then they saddle up three horses and head across the fields. I think Ben is maybe a little bashful when it comes to girls. But I think he probably thinks about me when he is alone. After all, if he didn't think about me at all, then he would acknowledge my presence the way he does Hershel's and Max's. The fact that he so studiously pretends not to see me must mean he doesn't want to betray the depth of his feeling. Just as I don't want yet to betray mine.

The Great Betrayal

That night in my pantry room, reading from the light of one dangling bulb, I hear the wolf howls again. They come down like a waterfall, tumbling toward us, echoing in silvery space, as if they have been poured over the moon. They raise gooseflesh on my arms, although I am not frightened of them. We are in a safe house, after all. It is they who are out there in the darkness.

Then I startle as my doorknob turns but it is not the wolves with newfound opposable thumbs, which is my first wild thought. It is only Maya. She clutches a blanket in one hand.

"Maya," I say, "did you drag the blanket off your bed all the way down here?"

She nods.

"Well, what's the matter?"

"I heard them," says Maya.

"The nonexistent wolves?" I ask.

She nods.

"Well, so? You know the whole ranch is fenced in, Maya. They can't get onto the ranchland so they can't get anywhere near the house."

"Suppose they get one of the horses?"

"The horses are in the barn. In their stalls." I say all this patiently because I am in a really good part of my book and I want her to go to bed.

"They could chew a hole in the fence," she says.

"Oh, for God's sake," I say.

"I don't want to sleep alone," says Maya.

"You're not sleeping alone. You're in a room with Dorothy."

"But her hip is broken," says Maya. "I want to sleep in here."

"My hip is broken too."

"I've never slept in a room without you," she persists.

This is true. I hadn't considered this, although I

did think about how this pantry is the first bedroom I have ever had to myself. I have rather en-
joyed it. I can keep the light on for hours if I like.
"Listen, Maya, I'm reading and I'm not turning off
the light for you."

She has already climbed into my bed.

"That's okay," she says, and closes her eyes. I
know she is going to pretend to be asleep. I go
back to reading.

"This is ridiculous," I say after a few minutes.
"There's no room in this bed. There's barely room
for me. Get out."

"I can't."

"You can too. Dorothy is there and Mama and
Ned are just down the hall. Go to bed."

"No."

"Maya, you're eight years old. You're old enough
to sleep in a room all alone, let alone next to Dorothy. Now GO TO BED!"

"No."

"What is the *matter* with you?"

"I saw wolf shadows on the wall in Dorothy's
room."

"Oh, you did not."

But Maya sits up in bed and suddenly her eyes are frightened and she says, while gripping my arm so hard she makes nail marks, "I DID. I hate it here. I want to go *home*."

"We are going to go home," I say. "You heard Mama. They just have to find some solution for Dorothy's living situation or something."

"She can come with us," says Maya.

"Listen," I say, because it suddenly occurs to me that no one has suggested this obvious solution and if Maya gets this notion into her head, she could create all kinds of embarrassment for my mother and Ned, who maybe don't want Dorothy to come with us. "I'm sure there's a reason why that wouldn't work and we shouldn't even talk about it. Now let's go to sleep."

I lie down and reach up to pull the string to turn the light off but she grabs my hand.

"Don't turn off the light," she says.

She turns her back to me but I can tell from just the *feel* of her that she is crying now. I find this worrying. Suppose, I think, that she gets home and she still isn't happy? Suppose there is something really *wrong* with her? My mother has said she thinks

Maya is fine, but maybe she is in denial. I don't really know enough about these things to know whether I should be worried about Maya or not but I don't *want* to be worried. So maybe I am in denial too. Maybe we should all look a little closer at her. But then I realize that if Maya is really in trouble we won't be able to stay here all summer and then I can't see Ben. That just makes me annoyed with her. I think that if Maya were really in trouble I wouldn't be able to be annoyed with her. So I must not, deep down, think she's in *real* trouble.

I forget about Maya's sniffling as I remember the way Ben looks, legs apart and braced, muscles tensed and ready, as he stands in the middle of the ring. I fall asleep thinking about this and never do get around to asking Maya why she is crying.

In the morning my mother opens the door. "Oh, here she is," she says. "I thought perhaps . . . Jane, come help me find Dorothy's car keys. I've mislaid them again."

While we look and Maya wakes up slowly in my bed, my mother says to me, "I'm going into town with Nelda to see about convalescent homes for Dorothy. Can you do something with Maya?"

"Like what?"

"See if you can get her interested in a book. Dorothy has a whole wall of them in the study. Maybe you can lure her away from the TV for a while, she just needs someone to play with."

I have not really checked out the books yet, fearing that they would all be *Reader's Digest* condensed versions like the few on the coffee table in the living room. But after we have eaten, I explore the study with Maya. There are no children's books for her and I'm beginning to get bored and itchy with dust when I see a bright cookbook. It is *The Julia Bestenmeyer Book of Candy Making*. There are bright pictures on every page of different kinds of candy. Saltwater taffy and peppermint drops. Chocolates. Hard candy, soft candy, fudge. And the women in the pictures all have pink-and-white-striped outfits and aprons. The candy is presented on pink-and-green cake plates. You never saw a happier venture. That Julia Bestenmeyer is one happy candy maker. And her message seems to be: Candy will make you happy. Just make some, you'll see.

I sit down in the comfortable overstuffed chair in the study and start to flip through it and to my surprise Maya comes and hangs over the chair, as mesmerized by such glossy candy happiness as I am.

"That would be fun," she says. "Making candy."

My mother comes in for her purse and over-hears. "That's a great idea. Jane, why don't you make candy with Maya? I'm sure Dorothy won't mind if you use her kitchen."

"Yeah, let's make candy!" says Maya, jumping up and down.

My mother and I smile. When was the last time we saw Maya excited about anything? Good. Maybe if I can keep Maya happy making candy we can stay here all summer.

"Okay," I say. "Let's make candy, Maya."

"See what supplies Dorothy has and I can take you shopping tomorrow for whatever else you need," says my mother, and speeds out the door.

The only thing we have all the right ingredients

for is plain pulled taffy but that looks like fun. Maya is bouncing all over the kitchen.

We spend the morning making the pulled taffy. We color it with the little food coloring that Dorothy has, some tiny drops of green and yellow and red. It reminds me a bit of the saltwater taffy we bought once on a road trip with Mrs. Parks, a woman from our church in Massachusetts. It is strange to think that Mrs. Parks is dead now. Beyond the reach of saltwater taffy.

Ned breezes through the kitchen, grabs a piece and burns his tongue. "OUCH. WARN people!" he says.

"Where are Hershel and Max?" I ask.

"Out in the ring. Ben is teaching them to ride. They hung over the ring looking pathetic enough until he got the hint and saddled up a couple of ponies for them."

I bristle in fury. He should be teaching *me*. *I've* hung over the ring looking longingly, winsomely and mysteriously at the horses. Clearly I should have gone for pathetic.

"Didn't Mom think they were too young for that?" I ask.

"Your mother thinks a lot of things," says Ned vaguely, and goes bustling on out again.

Maya and I clean up the taffy mess, which takes a while. It is a taffy that hardens as it cools so everywhere we dripped some is now rocklike and we have to scrape it and try to melt it off with hot dishrags. Then we arrange all the pieces on a cake plate. Hershel and Max come into the kitchen after their lesson. I don't want to give them any taffy. It's enough they get riding lessons. But they put their grubby little hands right into the taffy plate, smearing disgusting muddy red dust from the ring over it. "Oh, you gross animals!" says Maya when she sees.

They are unfazed and, after eating their fill, take some out to the barn for Hank and Leeron and Ben, of course, their new best friend.

Then Candace, looking all square-shouldered and businesslike, comes into the kitchen, where Maureen is sampling our candy, and announces she is going out to the barn to fire Leeron and Hank. Even though Ben is the youngest, he is the experienced ranch hand and the others work under him. I don't really mind her firing Leeron and Hank as long as she leaves Ben alone.

"Oh no!" says Maureen. "Not yet. We haven't made any provisions . . . we haven't told Mother. Let's wait, we've only just talked about it."

"No time like the present," says Candace briskly, scooping up a fistful of taffy. She puts a piece in her mouth and crunches it aggressively. I'm surprised she doesn't break a tooth. "I find if you wait around to do these things, they don't get done. 'Sign the papers! Sign the papers now!' I tell clients. That's why I'm one of the most successful realtors in my firm. I taught a seminar on closing and I talked for an hour and a half but this is what it could have boiled down to: CLOSE! CLOSE! Close the deal. *CLOSE!*"

Maya backs away from her and even I jump at this. Scary realtor. Scary realtor.

"I just think we should wait—" Maureen begins, but Candace gives her a look that says what a spineless jellyfish she thinks Maureen is, goes out to the barn and fires them. She comes in a few minutes later very pleased with herself as if being hard and unyielding is a talent.

For the next two days no one says anything to Dorothy about it. Even Candace doesn't seem to want to broach it. She has given Leeron and Hank until the end of the week so Dorothy doesn't even know they're fired until a few days later when Hank and Leeron go up to say goodbye to her and collect their wages and then we hear her scream, "SHE *WHAT?*"

Maya and I are in the kitchen making candy. We stop breathlessly as Candace, who has been drinking coffee on the porch, still basking in the glow of her decisiveness, goes upstairs to deal with it. We hear a lot of loud arguing and a lot of shrieking by Candace about how Dorothy can't afford to keep them on and Dorothy shrieking that it is none of Candace's business. Maya puts her hands over her ears.

"Come on, Maya," I say, because my mother is still driving around the state with Nelda looking for a decent living situation for Dorothy. They had no luck in Elko and are going off to check points west for convalescent homes and assisted-living facilities and will probably end up just combing the county for someone who takes in stray cats and is willing to expand to larger mammals.

There has been a shift in Maya the last day or so. She is neither irritable nor particularly interested in the candy. She just looks kind of blank. Now she is standing with her hands still over her ears and doesn't seem to hear when I tell her that the sugar we are boiling has reached the soft-ball stage. Usually she loves dropping hot balls of cooked sugar into cold water and seeing if you can squish them into a soft ball.

"Soft ball," I say again, showing her I have made one, but she doesn't even look. This turns my blood cold and then I think maybe I am being too dramatic. I decide to get her out of the house and away from the yelling, so I take her to the barn, where we can see what Max and Hershel are up to.

Hershel and Max, as usual, are leaping all over the barn. They tell us they are helping Ben load bales of hay onto a conveyor belt that takes it up to the loft. They don't appear to be much help, really. They spend a lot of time riding up the conveyor and jumping around in the hay and Ben yells at them frequently to stop stepping all over it.

He seems quite unfazed by Hank and Leeron's getting fired. I thought, given his clearly heroic persona, that he would threaten to quit in protest or at least appear to feel bad about it. But maybe he keeps his feelings bottled up. That could be why he never looks at me.

The boys tell Maya to ride up the conveyor but she says it is too scary. She goes up the ladder and finds a quiet corner of the hayloft until the boys wreak havoc again and Ben yells at them and then she goes back to the house. I follow behind her. Dorothy has stopped yelling at Candace, whose rented car is gone.

At least the house is quiet. Maya seems to forget that we are in the middle of candy making and goes to watch TV. My mother comes home. She and Nelda have had no luck with homes for Dorothy and they look tired and discouraged. I wish I had some candy to offer them. It was bright and cheerful. It perked everyone up while it lasted.

The next day my mom takes me and Maya grocery shopping in Elko. I have decided we should
branch out and make something truly exciting
like marshmallows. There is something so magical about homemade marshmallows and I am trying to reinterest Maya in the wonder of candy
making because I am slowly developing a plan to
be alone with Ben. If I can get Maya happily interested in cutting marshmallows into perfect
squares and decorating them with piped-on icing
flowers like the picture in the book, something
time-consuming enough that I can get out to the
barn, and if I can somehow get rid of Hershel and
Max, then I think I may have a shot at getting
Ben talking to me.

I am busily developing this plan as we go down
grocery aisles, when Maya grabs my shirt and
points. There is a bag of pastel-colored marshmallows. "Let's color them!"

Yes! This is a good sign. I've got her hooked
again.

We are in line at the grocery store with our load
of sugar and corn syrup and food coloring and
chocolate and sprinkles and other enticing candy

supplies when we overhear two women in front of us talking about the wolves.

"Well, Daran wants to take his rifle out and shoot them. They got one of Henry's sheep and who knows what they'll get next. I told the principal he'd better watch those children at recess."

"You can shoot them all as far as I'm concerned. There aren't supposed to *be* wolves in Nevada. Haven't seen them for years. I called Animal Control and they said that the closest ones are in Idaho. But lands, that's just over the border; you telling me wolves know a state line when they see one? They just don't want to deal with it. That's what that's about."

"Oh, and now they're on the endangered species list like everything else," says the cashier.

"Daran says what's the point of having a gun, you can hardly shoot nothing anymore, it's got so bad. Let's see how they feel when someone's horse gets mauled. I seen what a bear can do to a horse. My granny remembers wolf packs and she says let 'em be endangered. Good riddance to 'em."

"People seem to feel like Ben about them," I

whisper to my mother. "He wants to get rid of them too."

"I hope they have good places to hide," whispers my mother. "I would miss their calls."

Then it's our turn and we pay for all our stuff, and my mother drops us at home to cook and takes Nelda out again to look for homes. My mother isn't too crazy about all this activity on Dorothy's behalf, especially since Dorothy doesn't know about most of it. All she knows is that Hank and Leeron were fired. She doesn't know what else is in store for her. But my mother doesn't think it's her place to tell Dorothy any of this. It should come from her own children.

"Nelda can't drive so I feel duty bound to take her where she wants to go, but I feel funny about it," she says to Ned. "Shouldn't you be talking to Dorothy?"

"Someone should, I think Candace elected Nelda . . . ," says Ned and he is out the door so fast he leaves my mother saying into thin air, "But I don't think Nelda knows she was elected. . . . "

"Well, Jane," she says to me as we watch Ned disappearing round the side of the barn with the speed of light, "I guess I'll go tell Nelda it's time to go. I'm not sure when we'll get back."

I myself would find it very trying to spend a day carting Nelda around. Nelda never speaks above a whisper and so you're always having to say "What? What?"

This seems to really annoy Maureen, whose job it is to make breakfast and who gets her revenge by making jelly Madonnas on the toast. "There," she will say, "look at that, Nelda. You have a Madonna on your toast. It's a jelly miracle."

It all started one night at dinner when Nelda made the mistake of telling us about somewhere in Mexico where someone saw the Virgin Mary in a tortilla. People came from miles around to see the miracle. Everyone at the table scoffed at this except Nelda, who, it turns out, believes in these miraculous sightings. Maureen was particularly scathing and from then on miraculous sightings of the Virgin have appeared on Nelda's food. Last night Nelda found a Virgin Mary tomato configuration on her salad.

"Praise God," whispered Nelda when she sat down at her place and saw it.

"Praise Maureen, I made it, you ninny," said Maureen.

"I know," whispered Nelda, and ate it reverently all the same.

It's too bad they're all leaving soon. Just as we're getting to know them. But *que sera, sera*, it fits in perfectly with my plan. As if the universe aligns things so that Ben can observe me being saintly without the distraction of a lot of other people cluttering up the scenery.

I decide to make sheets of marshmallows and tell Maya we can't cut them and decorate them until just the right moment. Maya has taken to watching more and more TV with Dorothy. This would work fine except that lately Dorothy has had a tendency to send her to get snacks and her glasses and Kleenex and water and I am afraid Maya will drift down at a critical moment and see me out in the ring, come out and spoil *everything*.

Meanwhile my mother and Nelda, Maureen and Candace now all pile into three cars every morning, frantically trying to find a place that will take Dorothy. They have been told that sometimes it's just a matter of being at the right place at the right time. So much for waiting lists, says Candace. It gets my mother out of the way, though.

But what to do about the boys? They are annoyingly always around underfoot, or worse, under Ben's feet. Then, thank goodness, Max rips his last whole pair of jeans and my mother decides to take the boys into town to get them some pants.

As soon as I hear this I realize it is the best shot I am going to get at my plan. Ben is in the ring. The boys and my mother will be gone. My mother has sent Ned off to drive Nelda. Of course, my mother could have sent Ned shopping with the boys and driven Nelda but I bet she put her foot down and told Ned it was his turn to get whispered at all day.

I race into the kitchen, throw together some batches of different-colored icing and put it into paper decorating cones. Then I call upstairs. "Quick, Maya, the marshmallows are ready to be cut and decorated."

"I want to watch *The Price Is Right*," calls Maya.

"Well, you CAN'T!" I yell before I think of a

more tactful enticing way to put it. "That is," I go on, sounding very much like the witch in "Hansel and Gretel," "the marshmallows are all done and waiting, dear."

"They've been done for days," calls Maya.

"But the icing is HARDENING!" I screech.

Ned is futzing around outside talking with Ben while Nelda waits in the car.

I run upstairs and say, "Well, I can cut and decorate them myself, if you want. . . . "

Maya follows me downstairs with her blank look but I don't have time to think about her facial expressions.

"Okay, you can use this plastic icing knife to cut the marshmallows, see?" I say, demonstrating. "But they all have to be *exactly one inch square,* so measure each one with this ruler."

She nods. Good! Good, good, good. It makes sense to her. Of course, that means she is an idiot, but I can't worry about that now.

"Then you make a flower on *each* one with a little green, a little yellow and a little pink, just like the picture in the book. I'll show you."

I do a petal and run to the window. Good, Ben's

still there. Good, good, good. Will Ned *never* leave? I do a leaf, I run to the window.

"Okay, okay, I get it," says Maya, trying to grab the cone. "Why do you keep looking out the window?"

Why? Why, why, *why*? Ah! "I'm checking the *light levels*. Of course, the light levels."

"The *light levels*? What's that?"

"What is it? What is it? Easy. The *levels of light*!"

"Why?"

Why? Why, why, *why*? Ah! "*Too* much light will fade the marshmallows. Look how bright ours are, but one wrong beam of sunlight and they will end up looking like the pastel ones in the supermarket. We don't want *that*."

I race over and pull down all the blinds.

"Problem solved!"

"Do I have to keep the blinds closed?" asks Maya.

"Yes. Yes, yes, yes. Under no circumstances open the blinds! You don't want second-rate marshmallows. You want *perfect* marshmallows!"

"You're scaring me! Your voice is all weird."

"Don't be ridiculous!" I snap. Then I take a deep

breath. I am so close. Don't scare her now, I say to myself. Breathe, breathe. I take another deep breath. It makes me cough.

"Don't cough on the marshmallows," says Maya.

"I think the sugar is making me cough. I think I need to go outside and get some fresh air. You will have to start decorating alone. Do you think you can? I mean, I know you're only eight. . . . "

"I don't need you to help!" scoffs Maya. "I'm a better drawer than you."

"That's right, you are," I say soothingly. "You'll do great if you just follow a few simple instructions."

She nods.

"Okay, now remember to measure and remeasure all the marshmallows. You should end up with ninety-six," I say, pulling a number out of thin air. I stopped listening to myself several minutes ago. Has Ned left yet? Is it safe to go out? I peek out the window.

"Are the light levels still good?" asks Maya.

"PERFECT!"

She looks scared again so I take another breath.

"Ninety-six. Can you remember that?"

"I *get* it," says Maya. "Where are you going to be?"

"I don't know. Don't think about me, just think about the *marshmallows*, the *marshmallows*, Maya," I say to her, handing her the plastic knife.

I creep to the front door and peek out. The coast is clear. Good! Good, good, good. I am halfway across the yard, thinking Ned has left, when suddenly he comes out of the barn. Ben follows him. I quickly nip around the side of the barn and go in the back way. But they are coming back in. I hear their voices. I am standing by the hayloft ladder so I scamper up. I can wait in the loft until Ned finally takes off and then join Ben at the ring.

"We're going to have to sell the tack too," Ned is saying to Ben.

"Uh-huh," says Ben. Even the sound of his grunts is thrilling. I shiver. There is a space between floorboards and I can see them talking by the door.

"And Ben . . ." There's a pause. Ned is kicking some loose hay around.

Just go. Go already. Go, go, go!

"Why don't you give poor Jane a break and take her riding?"

Ben looks at Ned blankly as if he hasn't heard him.

"Oh, come on," wheedles Ned. "Anyone can see she's got a huge crush on you. Just give her a riding lesson."

Ben winces.

Revelation

How I get into the house after that is a blur. I stumble and knock over some hay bales and Ben runs up the ladder to investigate, sees me and looks blank. I go down the ladder and pass Ned, who says something indistinct, like "Aw, Bibles . . ." and something else I don't hear. I go into the house. I don't even remember passing Maya and I close myself off in my room. I lie on my bed with a roaring river in my head. All I can hear are the rushing waters but behind it I am stung with betrayal. Nothing I believed was true. The universe aligned nothing. Ned betrayed me. So insultingly. So patronizingly. So thoroughly. Ben thinks of me, all right, but not as I believed. He thinks of me as someone who makes him wince. All this passes in and out of my thoughts and then it is back to the nothingness of the roaring river.

Days pass.

My mother knows something is up. The tip-off is that every time Ned walks into a room, I walk out. Oh, why kid myself? Ned has told her. They tell each other everything. My mother gives me hugs absentmindedly every time I pass. It is the best she can do to show support without humiliating me further by letting me know she knows. Now, counting Ben, there are three people beside me who know my utter and complete humiliation. I am disgusting. So much so that the mere mention of me silences Ben. He cannot even address such a hideous notion. My feelings are so obvious that even Ned knows. He *pities* me. I am so inept that I need Ned to step in and beg Ben for favors. Ben probably already knew about my feelings. *That* is why he avoided me. I am loathsome and ugly and beneath his notice. And now he probably thinks I put Ned up to it.

I don't know what to do with my time that will keep me away from everyone. I could make candy with Maya but she is no longer interested. She didn't even finish making the marshmallows but, as I later found out, left a big half-finished mess in the kitchen, which my mother cleaned up when she came home.

"Come on, Maya, let's at least make nougat," I say enticingly, trying to reinterest her. "Look at the picture, all those colorful little bits of stuff stuck in the white candy. How, oh how, does one get the bits in there? Let us find out!"

"Why won't you let Ned have candy anymore?" she asks.

"Because he doesn't deserve it," I say.

"Why?" she persists.

"Because he's the devil's spawn."

After that Maya avoids Ned too. She has never been terribly chummy with him, regarding him with a certain amount of cool speculative detachment. He is a little too frivolous for her taste, I think. But now with the idea that he is the devil's spawn, she is keeping her distance. I feel vaguely guilty about giving her something else to feel frightened about. She sleeps in my room about two nights out of three as it is.

Then one night at dinner as Nelda quietly eats her sacred-apparition scalloped potatoes, Ned announces that he is thinking about going to Alaska.

"Ha!" says Dorothy. "Now, there's a surprise."

My mother has put down her fork and is looking at him with interest. Ned looks at her and his eyes drop guiltily.

"Listen, it's just so fascinating to me. The whole thing with John."

"So you thought you'd go when, Ned?" asks my mother.

"I don't know," said Ned. "Maybe when we get Dorothy settled."

"Before we drive back to Massachusetts?" asks my mother. Nobody looking at her would guess that this hasn't been their well-considered plan all along. She is eating her dinner as if they are discussing him going to get ice cream after dinner.

Dorothy has come down to dinner for the first time. She can't do stairs yet but she can shuffle a bit forward on her walker and Candace and Ned made a chair with their arms and carried her downstairs. She said it was a harrying ride and she did not plan to do that again. She seems quiet at dinner. As if she is saddened somehow by having all these grown offspring around the table. She sits next to Maya and they speak to each other in short, quiet half-sentences, as if during the few weeks we have been here they have developed their own code. Dorothy has been teaching her Abenglabish and sometimes they speak that instead.

"So you're going to go see Dad? Whew!" says Maureen. "Maybe we'll end up having a big family reunion someday after all. Wouldn't that be a kick?"

"Yeah," says Ned. "First I get to see my mother and sisters and now Dad and John. And I gotta find out the answers to some questions. Listen, it's all just so fascinating to me. I've been up night after night mulling it over. Why did John leave the money with the Carriers? This is what I've figured out. He must have been on his way to see Dad in Alaska when he discovered he was being followed. He's in B.C. when he suspects someone is hot on the trail of the money. And then he remembers that I'd stayed with the Carriers and so he scouts around, finds out where they live and leaves the money with them. Purportedly for me but really just a safe place to ditch it until he can come back for it."

My mother, who has been eating dinner and listening with interest, puts down her fork and nods. "Yes," she says. "It's the only explanation we have so far that makes sense. But of course you won't know for sure unless you talk to him."

"Exactly!" says Ned. "And then, of course, I'd want to return the money to him anyway. And, Mom, you don't want it around here when we leave."

"What money?" asks Candace, suddenly getting her business face again. It is more pronouncedly wrinkly than her regular face. "What's all this talk of money?"

"John left a bag of money," begins my mother, and stops. It's really a hard thing to explain.

"He *what?*" says Candace.

"A *bag* of money?" says Maureen.

"For who?" asks Candace.

Nelda is still working on the Virgin. Maybe she is too devout to take any interest in bags of money.

"It's a long story. The thing is to return it," says

Ned. "I mean, we're not saying it's hot or anything, but who knows where it came from? Best thing is to get it back to him."

"Can't they tell if it's hot by feeling it?" asks Max.

"He means stolen," I say to Max.

"You and Ned are outlaws," says Max.

"No, we're not," I say.

"Outlaws!" says Hershel, and he and Max bounce in their chairs and pretend to shoot pistols around the table, saying "Bang bang bang!"

"Oh, shut up," I say. My mother looks at me but I am all the way down at the other end of the table.

"You're just going to go to Alaska and start *looking for him?*" asks Candace as if she cannot believe her ears. "You could be gone for *years.*"

"I don't think it would take so long. There aren't that many people in Alaska. . . . " Ned is very interested in his pork roast suddenly.

"*There aren't that many people in Alaska?*" Candace echoes.

"Well, after we have Mother moved into the facility, of course."

"After you have Mother moved *WHERE?*" shrieks Dorothy, suddenly coming fully awake and alive.

"NED!" says Maureen.

"Oh honestly, Ned," says Candace, throwing her napkin down on the table. "Nelda was going to break it to her tactfully."

"Tactfully my eye. Now, just what do the four of you have cooked up?" asks Dorothy.

I notice she leaves my mother out of this. I am glad. My mother was never too thrilled about the whole plan from the beginning.

"Mom, we wanted to wait until we found a place . . . ," begins Maureen.

"Someplace nice," says Nelda in her squeaky little soft voice.

"*Someplace nice?* Now wait a cotton-pickin' minute," says Dorothy. "I may have lost the use of my hip but not my mind. I can find my own nice places, thank you very much."

"HOW?" asks Candace. "How can you find your own nice place? You can't ever walk properly again."

"How do you plan to go? Do you fly and we drive back or do you drive and we fly back to

Massachusetts?" asks my mother as if she hasn't heard anything else going on at the table. It is the one and only sign that Ned's news about Alaska has distressed her because it is so unlike her to tune out others.

"I can never *walk* again?" asks Dorothy, but this time as if she can barely breathe.

"Well, I'd have to use some of the money from the bag, of course, as expenses, but I guess I would fly, yes . . . ," says Ned.

"Candace!" says Nelda in a loud whispery voice.

"Oh honestly," says Maureen. "Mom, this is coming out all wrong. The doctor wanted us to tell you. He seems like a nice man and he thought we could do it better. . . ." She stops as it occurs to everyone how wrong he was. "But yeah, you damaged some vertebrae and at your age . . ."

"So this is it, this is as good as it's going to get?" asks Dorothy.

"Which is why you're going to need help. You know, they have very nice places with a staff who can help you."

"Great balls of fire!" says Dorothy.

"Now, there's no need to react like that. You have no idea what we've been through trying to find you a nice place before we went home," says Candace, bending her napkin into neat little folds. "And luckily today we finally found one by Ely that will take you, and when we sell the ranch you'll have enough money to pay for it for some time."

Dorothy looks too stunned to speak.

Maya hasn't been following the conversation among the sisters and Dorothy. She has had her ears glued to my mother and Ned and now she leans over and whispers to Dorothy but in tones loud enough for us all to hear, particularly as her whisper echoes in the great stunned silence. "You were right. About *you know who* . . ." She points at Ned behind her napkin but of course we all see this too.

"What have you been telling her?" Ned barks at Dorothy in outraged tones.

"Just the truth. I thought she should know. Now, you're a very nice boy, Neddie, but you're not reliable. I didn't want her getting too attached."

"Too *ATTACHED*!" says Ned.

"Dorothy, honestly," says my mother. "Ned is very reliable."

"He's going to *Alaska!*" says Dorothy.

"Well, yes, . . . there *is* that," says my mother musingly.

"Too *ATTACHED?*" Ned is almost standing in indignation. He throws his napkin on the floor.

"Jane thinks he's the devil's spawn," whispers Maya confidingly to Dorothy, but unfortunately we all hear this too.

My mother looks over at me wild-eyed. I know she counts on me to support her but, honestly, she *knows* what he did to me. I roll my eyes and start looking for my own scalloped-potato Virgin Mary.

"Anyhow, Mother, you can't stay on here alone and we can't stay and take care of you," says Maureen. "So obviously some kind of living situation had to be found."

"Well, I never!" Dorothy sputters. "What were you planning to do . . . just up and move me one day without warning?"

"That's just what *you* did," says Nelda quietly without looking up. "That's just what you did with us. You moved us all to Fort McMurray, where nobody wanted to go. You just moved us without warning."

"Oh, *that's* what this is all about. For heaven's sakes," says Dorothy. "That was all years ago. So this is just revenge."

"Don't be ridiculous," says Maureen, but it suddenly occurs to me that maybe this is what this *is* all about. And from the look on Maureen's face, this is occurring to her too.

"That's *not* what this is about," says Candace. "This is purely practical. We're just looking for a place for you, is all. We're trying to help you here."

"Well, thanks for telling me because I never would have guessed that throwing me out of my own home was particularly helpful. Ned, take me upstairs. I want to go back to bed."

But Ned is turning to me instead. "Jane, I'm sorry. I don't know how many ways to say it. It just slipped out. I didn't know you'd take it so hard. I mean, it's nothing to be ashamed of, having a crush on a boy."

Thank you very much, Ned. Now there are eight people who know. That was *so* helpful.

"Ned," says my mother. "Let's not talk about that here."

"Who does Jane have a crush on?" asks Maya.

"Is Jane going to crush someone?" asks Max.

"Who is Jane going to crush?" asks Hershel.

"NOBODY!" I yell.

The aunts are studiously looking elsewhere. Oh great! Everyone *already* knew!

"Nobody tells *me* anything," says Maya in aggrieved tones.

"Can we have dessert?" asks Max.

"Yes, come, boys, let's go into the kitchen and I'll get you dessert," says my mother.

"Take me to bed," says Dorothy. "I'll admit I may have to move somewhere where someone will assist me *now that I know I'll never be able to walk properly again* but I don't have to put up with you all planning it behind my back like I'm senile. Honest to God. Sometimes I wish I'd had gerbils instead when the mothering instinct came over me."

"*What* mothering instinct?" Maureen whispers to Nelda, but we all overhear that too. When are people going to learn that you can hear almost any whisper at the dinner table? Even though Dorothy is halfway out the door, being carried by Candace and Ned, I think she hears too because her body becomes rigid.

My mother comes into the dining room. "Pie, anyone?"

We all shake our heads. We are either angry or in the depths of inconsolable despair.

"It's pecan . . . ," says my mother.

"Well, maybe just a slice," says Maureen.

"Yes, a sliver," whispers Nelda.

"A crumb," says Candace.

"Oh well, if it's pecan . . . ," I say, and sullenly let her bring it to me.

Bye-bye

The next day Ned announces that he and his sisters are going to take Dorothy to see the home in Ely that has space for her.

"We'll make a day of it," says Maureen to Dorothy, who has been gotten dressed and is sitting stonily at the breakfast table clutching her patent leather pocketbook as if she might swipe anyone who came near.

"We can stop in Ely for lunch," says Candace.

"If you think that's supposed to be an inducement then you've obviously never eaten out in Ely," says Dorothy.

Ned comes downstairs and he and Dorothy and the sisters take off.

I wash the breakfast dishes. It is soothing work.

Maya is curled up in Dorothy's bed watching television. She has gone back to putting her knuckles by her mouth. I think the amount of discord in the house is upsetting her. I am loafing about the study dipping into Dorothy's dusty old books when my mother comes in.

"So, want to go riding, just you and me?" she asks.

"I don't know how," I say.

"I do," she says. "And with a nice gentle trail horse, you don't need to know. Your horse can just follow mine."

"I didn't know you could ride," I say.

"Yes. A little," says my mother. "And Dorothy told me she has a very gentle old mare that used to do trail rides and that if you're on her, you should have no trouble. I've asked Ben to keep an eye on the boys and I've told Maya that Ben is just in the barn with them if she needs anything. I've already got the horses saddled up and tied by the gate so we can just take off."

Without having to pass by Ben, I suppose she means. This all begins to sound very suspicious to me. She is probably trying to get me alone so she can tell me that I have to forgive Ned and then she will try to plead his case. It annoys me. It's not like my mother to be such a buttinski. She ought to be as mad at him as I am. We should form an anti-Ned club. I think I may point this out to her. Maybe she is just waiting for someone to give her license to be mad at him.

I get on the horse and at first the novelty of this wipes out all thought.

We ride slowly out over the grasslands. The sky is light washed blue with clouds painted in patches. The grass pokes from the earth so that there is almost an equal amount of both and you can see mountains in the background. The air is thin and dry and coated with a fine haze of dirt so that you have it not just under your feet but filtering into your lungs in a way that is pleasant. The way the earthy smell of the manure pile is pleasant.

This country is twice as beautiful on horseback. For the first time I feel like I am part of the landscape. It is what I always feel on our beach in Massachusetts. That I am an integral part of it. I wonder if everyone finds home like that or if some people,

like Ned, never do. And so they're not even looking for it, they just keep moving.

Out of habit, the thought that I am finally on
horseback like an outlaw crosses my mind but I
quickly correct it. No more being outlaws with
Ned. Well, we never were, I think he just wanted
to get away from things. I wanted adventures to
get *to* things. This is the difference I could never
put my finger on.

We ride side by side and don't talk at all. The
gentle rocking of the horse is soothing and my
mother looks awake and alive and happy in a way
I realize I haven't seen her for a long time.

I would love it if Ned went to Alaska. But I
am doubly angry at him, now on my mother's
behalf, for wanting to do so. Suppose he goes
and she never looks peaceful like this again? Suppose she becomes like Dorothy when Ned's father
left?

"I'm sorry to say it but I think Ned is doing a
really terrible thing wanting to go to Alaska like
that. I think he's really"—I am hesitant to be so
harsh about my mother's husband but she should
at least have the idea suggested to her—"not a very

good person after all. At the very least, he is doing a *bad* thing."

My mother looks at me and she doesn't lose her placidity. She looks neither angry at Ned nor at what I have said. "Most things we think other people do that are bad are merely inconvenient for us, Jane. Most people we think are bad have just not acted in a way that was convenient *for us*. We assume they must have evil reasons if they do things that don't turn out well for us, but most of the time we just don't get it." She shrugs.

I am flustered by this. I still want to think of Ned as bad. I don't want to think of all these complications so I change the subject. "Have you noticed that Maya has been a little weird lately?"

"I've noticed you watch her with a worried expression," says my mother. "She'll be much better when we get home and she makes a friend."

"Do you really think that's it?" I say hintingly. I don't want to worry her but maybe she ought to at least think about these things. "You know I was watching *The Price Is Right* with her and Dorothy for a few minutes and there was a commercial. With the six signs of depression."

"And you thought Maya had some?"

"She had *all* of them," I say.

My mother reins in her horse, turns to me and smiles. "Maya's going to be okay, Jane. Even with her family history of mental illness, it never occurred to me she'd be anything else. She's sensitive and she's going through changes. As we all are. Sometimes when people are going through changes you just have to give them space to make them. But she's solid. Just wait and see."

All this business about changes goes right over my head because of the arresting first thing my mother said. *What* family history of mental illness? There is no mental illness on my mother's side of the family. She must mean Maya's *father's* family history. This is the first time my mother has ever made any reference to any of our fathers and I think it just slipped out.

Back in Massachusetts I managed to figure out four men who were probable fathers of my brothers and sister and me, assuming each one of us had a different one. But I was never sure which man had fathered each of us. Which one of them had mental illness in the family?

Which potential father had a family *history* of mental illness? Immediately Crazy Caroline springs to mind, sister of a poet who I thought might have fathered one of us. That is the obvious answer. And she really was crazy. Certifiably, sadly, frighteningly crazy. That would make the poet, H.K., Maya's father.

The rest of the ride is ruined for me. I look in the direction of my mother's hands, pointing out hawks and vultures and snakes and dust devils, but I can't care. How I long for my best friend, Ginny, back in Massachusetts. For someone who will be-have normally when I tell her that Maya's father is H.K. and Ned wants to desert us all and go to Alaska and there's a bag of money sitting in the house and one of Ned's sisters believes the Virgin Mary appears to people in waffles and how Ned betrayed me with Ben, and about Ben, and who, when I tell her these things, doesn't just sit there smiling serenely but runs around in circles like a chicken with her head cut off, screaming, "OH MY GOD! OH MY GOD! OH MY GOD!" Now, *that* is what is called for. *That* would be satisfying. But there is no such person here.

Later, as we turn the horses for home, it occurs to me that just as momentous as knowing that H.K. is most likely Maya's father, is that by discovering this, I narrow down the possibilities of my own. The man who fathered me must now be one of the three remaining: Mr. Fordyce, who lives in a trailer outside of our town in Massachusetts and looks like Santa Claus; the clothes hanger man, whom I alone saw drown; or, and here I shiver with revulsion, Ned.

"Where were you?" demands Maya after we have untacked the horses and come onto the porch. She stands in the doorway with her hands on her stubby little hips.

"We went for a ride," I say.

"You didn't tell me you were going *horseback riding*," says Maya.

"Maya, you don't even like horses," I remind her tiredly.

"Nobody ever tells me anything," pouts Maya.

Sweetie pie, I want to say to her, you don't know the half of it.

Maya

When Ned and his sisters return they are chipper. They have found an assisted-living facility with a vacancy. Dorothy can move in anytime.

"It's a dump," says Dorothy at dinner. "But I guess my presence will improve it."

"That's the spirit, Mom," says Candace.

Dorothy smiles. She seems pathetically anxious to spend what time she has left with her returned children before they leave again. She is amiable at the cost of doing this thing she really doesn't want to do, moving to assisted living. It is better than being on the outs with them. I know this because Dorothy confides in Maya, who confides in me.

"It was the best we could do, Mother," says Nelda.

"You're lucky we found *that*," says Candace.

"My God, what do the old people *do* around here?" says Maureen, clucking her tongue and loading up her plate. That things are settled and they can all leave now has clearly given her a hearty appetite.

"Anyhow," says Candace to my mom, filling her in on the details of the day, "they have one nice apartment available but expect two even nicer ones to be available soon. They said they can't be sure exactly when, of course. But if you and Ned can hang out here awhile longer—it might not be until August, although probably no later, they said—then she can get into something better."

"Of course we'll stay until she can get into the nicer apartment," says my mother.

"I don't get it," says Dorothy. "Why don't they know exactly when these people are moving out? Don't they have to give some kind of notice?"

The silence at the table is deafening and then Dorothy says, "Oh, oh my, oh yuck. They've got a couple of people dying whose rooms are going to be available." She drops her fork and looks ill.

"In such cases, Mother," says Nelda, "it is perhaps best to be pragmatic and not think sentimentally."

"Oh dear," says Dorothy. "You just wait until you're my age, you'll think 'sentimentally' too. I suppose someday someone will be hoping I die quickly so they can get *my* apartment."

"Mom, please . . . ," says Candace.

"Well, anyhow, I suppose that means you're all going now?"

"Aren't you glad that Ned and Felicity can stay and help?" asks Maureen. "Goodness, these days with everyone working, it's hard to find someone who can uproot themselves like that. You ought to be grateful."

"Thank you," says Dorothy. She looks a little sad and lost and the sisters, I notice, make an effort to keep up a cheerful flow of inconsequential conversation after that. Maya reaches over and holds Dorothy's hand through the rest of dinner. I see Dorothy clutching it in her lap.

The sisters are going at the end of the week and in the meantime we are all kept busy by the impending ranch sale and move. I am helping my mother and Candace pack boxes of things Dorothy wants to take and arrange for the sale of other things. Dorothy wants to have a garage sale of smaller items while she is still at the house and can supervise the pricing. She is sure that left to our own devices we would undersell her things. My mother thinks it is only fair that Dorothy have as much control of this whole mess as possible. She and Ned and I bring things into her bedroom and let her set the prices and then carry them out to the barn, where we have set up tables.

"Suppose I am fine in a few months?" says Dorothy. "Then what?"

"Then you change your plans, Mom," says Ned, shrugging. "Life is plastic. You can always change your plans."

"Yes, look at you, you're going to Alaska as soon as you can dump me in a home," says Dorothy.

"Ned," says Candace as the three of us go down the stairs with armloads of overpriced knickknacks, "you shouldn't say things like that to her. You're just giving her false hope. You know the doctor said that she won't walk unassisted ever again."

"Aw, those guys don't know everything. Besides, what's wrong with a little false hope? And you know she's going to be easier to deal with if she thinks she's got something to look forward to. Well, anybody would be," he says fairly. "And I'm the one who's gotta put up with her. You're leaving at week's end."

Candace sighs and puts her things down on the table in the barn and says, "Well, maybe you're right. Speaking of which, I got you a little going-away present." Out of her pocket she pulls a cell phone.

"Aw, man, I hate these things," says Ned, putting down his own load and wiping his hands on his jeans before reaching for it. I have walked out. I am still avoiding being around Ned too much in case I am sucked into conversation. But I pause outside the barn door. Eavesdropping is not beneath me.

"I know, I know," says Candace swiftly, "but never mind. How can you, with any integrity, go to Alaska unless Felicity can reach you?"

"Well, I suppose that's thoughtful of you," says Ned, sounding surprised.

"Or in case Mom or one of us has to reach you, if there's a problem with Mom and someone, *someone without a job*, needs to come back and tend to it," says Candace, and Ned makes a face.

"Yeah, right," he says sourly.

Candace goes on as if he hasn't said anything, looking perfectly efficient and pleased with herself. "And you ought to get one for Jane in a year or so. All the teenagers have them now. They all go around texting each other. It's like jungle drums."

"It makes me want to throw up," says Ned.

"Well, who cares what you want to do? I'm giving another one to Felicity to keep in her purse."

"Uh-huh," says Ned, and tucks it in his back pants pocket.

"Will you keep it on?"

"Probably not," says Ned. "It sounds expensive. You have to buy some sort of a plan for these things, don't you?"

"Not for this one. I got you a pay-as-you-go plan and I've loaded up several months' worth of minutes for you. So you're all set."

"Oh jeez, thanks," says Ned. "Now I'm available to you at a moment's notice, I guess. How convenient for you."

"I've never seen anyone accept a present so graciously," says Candace.

"Face it, this is more like a present for *you*," says Ned.

"You *use* it," says Candace. "You *use* it or I'm flying to Alaska and . . . and . . . doing *this*." She reaches up and tweaks his ear. It is surprisingly playful for her and it is as if the years have dropped away and this is how they would have been if things hadn't gone so wrong when their father ran out on them. Then I wonder if this playfulness is because she is simply relieved to be leaving.

"Ow," says Ned, and starts to say something, but just then the boys come running through the barn, charging with pitchforks and followed by Ben, who is yelling at them to put them down. I speed into the house.

We have to work like crazy to get things ready for Saturday's garage sale. Dorothy, when not pricing things, sinks into long sleeps. She doesn't seem interested in watching TV with Maya very much anymore. She is always sleeping.

When Ned has any free time at all, you can find him on the living room couch with a stack of Alaska guidebooks. Maya comes into the kitchen when I am supposed to be packing pots and pans and hangs around getting in my way so I tell her to go talk to Ned. She surprises me by immediately going into the living room and plopping herself on the couch. I can see her from my seat on the floor.

"When are you getting back from Alaska?" asks Maya.

"I don't know, Mayie, sometime," says Ned vaguely.

"Well, when?" asks Maya.

"Maya, I'm trying to read," says Ned.

So Maya tries to hang out with the boys for the rest of the week but they gang up on her in one of their silly games that is more fun for them than for her. Maya finally has enough and seeks out Ned.

"Max and Hershel keep hitting me with the lasso. They say I have to be the cow and they're the rodeo stars," Maya says. "Make them stop."

"Make them stop making you the cow?" says Ned, and laughs.

This infuriates Maya, who goes stomping out of the barn, where we are, as ever, carrying and arranging things for the next day's sale.

"Oh, Maya, lighten up!" Ned calls. "I wasn't making fun of you, it just sounds so funny."

At lunch Maya says she is ready to make candy again.

"I can't, Maya," I say. "I promised Mama I would help them get ready for the sale. Why don't you help too?"

"I don't want to," she says. "Why do we have to stay? Why couldn't Candace stay? I want to go home."

"Everyone wants to go home but the others all have jobs to go back to."

"Nobody will play with me," says Maya. "Why did Mama go for a horseback ride with you and not me?"

"Maya, for heaven's sake!" I yell. "Stop whining! You don't even like horses!"

I am covered in dust, which I am allergic to. I don't want to be here either, carrying endless loads into the barn, avoiding Ned and Ben.

We don't see Maya again until dinner and then she is quiet. She doesn't sleep in my room that night.

···········

The day of the garage sale is crazy. People start arriving at seven o'clock, before we have even had breakfast.

"Oh my gosh, look at the crowds," says my mother to Ned. "Who would think there were so many people in Nevada? The ad said the sale didn't start until nine. What are they all doing here at this hour?"

"I guess they figure the early bird gets the worm," says Ned, grabbing a cup of coffee and heading outside. "I'm going to let them in. After all, if we want to sell this stuff, the earlier we get rid of it, the earlier we can quit."

After that we are all kept on the run. Ben is watching the boys. Dorothy has told him that she will put the sale of the horses in his hands and he can stay on until the ranch is sold and she moves into the home.

Around noon my mother goes in to put lunch out for everyone to grab when they get a chance. She gives me a tray to take to Dorothy, who is asleep as usual. "Jane, have you seen Maya?" my mother asks when I return to the kitchen.

"No, she's probably sulking somewhere," I say.

"Well, can you check for me?" she asks, heading back to the crowds in the barn.

"Sure," I say.

I look around the house but don't see Maya and I am about to check the outbuildings when I am buttonholed by a man who wants to know if we will take a quarter for a bronze horse statue priced at twenty dollars and I have to say no and he starts to argue with me, and another woman comes up and offers ten dollars for it and I get drawn back to work, despite myself, and the rest of the day passes in a blur.

At dinner we all drag exhaustedly to the kitchen table. My mother throws eggs into a pan, makes a giant omelet and then says, "Where did you find Maya, Jane?"

"I didn't," I say, sitting at the kitchen table sucking on an orange. "I got sidetracked."

Ned comes bursting into the kitchen. "We made twelve hundred dollars," he says. "That includes some tack that Ben couldn't sell in town."

"Have you seen Maya, Ned?" asks my mother, frowning and putting more bread in the toaster.

"She's probably with Dorothy," he says.

"Jane, could you check?" asks my mother but her voice is strained. She wipes a tendril of hair off her sweaty forehead. I can't understand why she is worried. Maya can't go far. There's nowhere to go. But Dorothy is asleep again and Maya isn't with her. I look all over the house. Ned goes out to check the barn. Candace, Nelda and Maureen scour the outbuildings. Everyone starts calling for Maya but she isn't answering.

Dorothy wakes up and doesn't improve matters by shuffling to the top of the stairs and calling down, "Phone the sheriff! All those people here today with their cars. Anyone could have snatched her."

"Mom, stop," says Ned. But now he looks worried. My mother says no, she doubts that Maya was kidnapped, but where could she be?

We all forget dinner. Now *I* am worried. My mother and I are looking together again through the barn when Ben comes in. She explains what we are doing and he says he will saddle up and start riding the property in case she has wandered off.

Just then we hear the wolves.

"Darn it, I'm going to *shoot* those things," says Ben, throwing an unsold saddle onto Satan. He can tack up a horse with lightning speed and is galloping off within minutes.

"Do you think a wolf ate her?" asks Max, his eyes like saucers.

"NO, MAX," I say.

"No, Max," says my mother, picking him up, something she hasn't done in a long time, but I think she just wants to hold someone. "Now, let's just calm down and think. Let's think where she might have gotten to."

We are standing there and Ned comes in to say he's checked the truck and the car and she's not there either. Ned is looking frantic now. "It's just that you can usually predict where she will be. This isn't like her to be nowhere."

"Exactly," says my mother. "Did something special upset her?"

"No one would play with her," I say.

My mother frowns.

"She's had enough," says Ned. "She wanted to go home a long time ago. This is all my fault. We never should have come here. We should have taken her home."

My mother is opening her mouth to speak when we hear Ben galloping back at a furious rate and we all run into the yard to meet him.

"There's a break in the fence," he says breathlessly. "And wolf tracks."

"Did you see the wolves?" asks Ned.

"No, it looks, actually, from the tracks like they headed out again the way they came in."

"I'm saddling up too," says Ned. "I think we'd better scour the grounds anyhow. Don't worry, Felicity. I'm sure she's hiding somewhere in the house where we just haven't found her. Maybe she fell asleep there."

We go inside and my mother paces and then she starts checking the house and grounds again and calling for Maya. She can't seem to stop moving.

When Ned gets back he is pale. They've found nothing. But now he has seen the wolf tracks too.

We have gone out to the ring, where Ben has tied up the saddled horses in case they are needed again, and Ned keeps saying, "Darn it, I don't like seeing those wolf tracks."

"Shhh, shhh," says my mother, who is still holding Max, who starts to cry.

For a second I think of Maya's mangled wolf-eaten body lying somewhere and I unexpectedly tear up and then tilt my head back to hide it. That's when I see the hayloft.

"Did anyone look up in the hayloft?" I ask.

My mother is already halfway up the ladder by the time the rest of us get into the barn. We follow her up and when we reach the top we see her sitting on the floor in the hay, holding Maya in her lap. Maya's face is pale and listless and she has her fist halfway in her mouth. She looks miserable. Who knows how long she has been up here like this? Who knows why she didn't come down when she heard us? We stare at her, our eyes huge, all except for my mother's, which are closed.

Ned says, "Enough of this. We're going home."

After that we all go back to the house. Not even Dorothy comments on us going home or the new arrangements that will have to be made. Or that Ned has changed his mind about Alaska.

We all go to bed. Maya falls right asleep. But I stay awake, thinking about Ned's new plan. My mother hasn't reacted to it any more than she did his plan to go to Alaska. They are on the porch swing and I can hear them through my window. But they don't seem to have much to say. All I hear are things like "Jeez." "Yeah." "Christ." "Yeah." "Never want to do that again." "Nope." And the sound of the porch swing creaking well into the night.

The next night at dinner we sit around the dinner table talking about what has to be done now that we are leaving as well.

"Well," Candace begins. "You're still going to have to do something about that money. You can't just deposit it. Not that amount. Maybe the best thing is to turn it over to the police."

"Aw, Candace, we'll be here forever explaining things if we do that," says Ned.

"Maybe we should split it between us. Not to keep, I mean," says Nelda in her whispery voice. "Just to hang on to temporarily. In smaller amounts it won't be so suspicious."

"I don't want anything to do with that money, thank you," says Candace. "That money is trouble. Maybe you *should* bring it to Alaska, Ned."

"I've already told you that I'm not going to Alaska," said Ned.

"Never mind the money, any of you," says Dorothy suddenly, and she is usually so quiet at these meals that it startles all of us. "*I'm* keeping it. I'm going to stay on at the ranch and use it to pay Ben to care for me. I don't need nursing, I just need help with things like shopping and driving and cooking and such."

"Mom . . . ," says Maureen. "How can you stay on here? We've already sold so much of your stuff."

"Don't need much," says Dorothy.

"Since when?" says Candace. "And I thought you didn't want this money any more than I did. Than any of us did."

"I didn't but then was then and now is now. You don't know how it's been preying on my mind, having to turn Ben out. He's been a good ranch hand and he's been good to me and this is all he knows. It wouldn't be so easy for him finding another job in these parts. Now I don't need to sell Satan either. Ben can care for him, do my chores and my shopping, and I can stay here until the money runs out. I figure that money will buy me two more years on the ranch."

"Well, gee, Mom," says Maureen.

"I still say it's risky. You don't know who is after that money," says Candace.

"Well, life's a risky business," says Dorothy. "Besides, for all we know no one is after that money. All we really know about it is that John left it for Ned to take care of. I've made up my mind. I made it up the second you told me Ned wasn't going to Alaska."

Ned and his sisters look at each other around the table and then Ned shrugs. "Okay, then, suit yourself," he says. "Go tell Ben."

"Already have," says Dorothy complacently. "Pass the peas."

············

The rest of the week is spent preparing to leave. Ben is going to move into the house when we go. Ned gives him his new cell phone number. He gives it to Dorothy too.

"May come in handy after all, Bibles," he says to me, but I am still ignoring him.

Ben has been going back and forth doing airport runs with the sisters, who leave one by one until it is just us.

Finally we say our goodbyes. Everyone is dry-eyed and overly cheery but Maya, who lingers behind when the rest of us go down to the car. She looks sad but I know that she is as anxious to get home as the rest of us. Finally she comes down too.

Ben is outside piling leftover tack and tools into the truck. He will probably try to sell it in town.

"He seems very reliable," says my mother reassuringly as we drive away.

"I think he is," says Ned. "I sure hope so."

"I still feel kind of bad about leaving Dorothy after we said we'd stay," says my mother.

"Aw, she's okay," says Ned. He is going into his meditative driving state. You can always tell. His answers get shorter and he begins to sound far away.

"It seems so odd. I was mentally prepared to be here for the summer and suddenly we are leaving. I haven't quite digested it. I feel like we didn't give Dorothy time to digest it properly either."

"She won't mind, I'm telling you, she's not attached that way," says Ned, and we drive quietly after that.

It is a subdued ride across the country.

One night as we drive and Maya and the boys sleep, my mother says to Ned that she keeps thinking about when Dorothy said to him not to worry about her, to "get that little girl home."

"It's so funny," says Ned, "how different she is with Maya than she ever was with us as kids. How she puts her first."

"Well, they say people are different with their grandchildren," says my mother.

"Stepgrandchild at that," says Ned, shaking his head.

I make a mental note of this, more evidence that he isn't Maya's biological father.

············

When we get back to the beach it is a wonderful salty homecoming. The moist air makes
me come alive. I can feel it seeping into all
my pores, which were shriveled in the desert
dryness. It is as if I can finally breathe all over
my body again, in my skin, my blood vessels,
my brain. The first few days we do nothing
but hang out on the beach. It is like a miracle
to hear the waves crash and recede, crash
and recede as they have been doing all this
time while we were gone. It felt oddly that we
stopped their movement by going away but we
never did.

I love everything here with renewed vigor. The
salt marshes. The loons serenely paddling through
the long grasses. The crickets at night. The stars
over the ocean. The village with its whitewashed
buildings. Our tiny two-room church with its
pointy steeple. The air-washed salt-faded colors of
the clothes of people who live by the shore. Our
laundry line. The creak in the floorboards on the

left side of the porch. Waking up to luminous dawn.

Ginny is still at camp but I am patient, knowing I will see her before long and be able to tell her everything.

The house is immaculate and it is soon apparent why. Mrs. Merriweather, a woman from our church, comes over when she hears we are returned.

"My dear!" she says to my mother, sitting happily across the table from her and shoveling in my mother's freshly baked cookies. "How happy we all are to find you safely back. The place was not the same without you. Not the same at all!"

"What happened to the Gourds?" asks my mother. "You wrote that they had vacated our house but you didn't say why."

"Did no one tell you? Well! Therein lies a tale. While Mr. Gourd was in prison, Mrs. Gourd took up with a young muscleman—really, I know no other term for him—from Lincoln. Lifted weights all the livelong day. Worked somewhere, I don't know where, but he'd come around here in his souped-up Trans Am with the engine running, revving it in the parking lot while she and those children hurried across the beach to him. The fumes, my dear, the fumes! And the noise! Well, anyhow, they were dating for only a month or so and the week before Mr. Gourd got out of prison, they left."

"What? They left town?"

"Yes. She pulled those children right out of school and loaded them into that Trans Am and off they took. And to where, do you think?"

"I have no idea!" says my mother.

"None other than Venice, California. And why? Because Mr. Muscleman wanted to lift weights on Muscle Beach. Have you ever? Have you ever heard of a sillier reason for moving an entire family cross-country than that?"

My mother shakes her head no.

"Of course, people say it was also to avoid Mr. Gourd, who was bound to come back for her. But she had complete custody of those children, so she could do as she liked. I'm afraid she found in the new boyfriend all the qualities she thought she'd left behind with Mr. Gourd. Really, it makes you wonder if people ever learn anything."

"Yes, it does," says my mother, round-eyed, eating another cookie herself.

"Well, as soon as I heard they'd flown the coop I came right over here and, my dear, the mess. It would have broken your heart."

"Mess?" says my mother. "The place is immaculate."

"Yes, after we got done with it. Some of us from church showed up with our mops and buckets and soon put things to rights, no thanks to those messy Gourds. Jam everywhere!"

"And peanut butter, I bet," I say, pulling up a chair.

"Oh, you may be sure," says Mrs. Merriweather, nodding at me. "Peanut butter everywhere! Oh, and you've not heard about Mrs. Spinnaker either, I suppose?"

"I notice she doesn't seem to be here this summer."

"No. Nor anywhere. Her sister has been frantic. She's gone and Horace is gone. They've been missing six months now. Her sister is putting the cottage up for sale. She fears"—and here Mrs. Merriweather whispers even though it is clear she would like everyone in the world to hear—"that Mrs. Spinnaker has come to a *bad end!*"

"No!" says my mother. "What *kind* of a bad end?"

"Well, my dear, the last anyone saw of her was during the winter storms. We had some doozies around New Year's. Waves fifteen feet high. Mrs. Spinnaker showed up for the holidays—something she has never done before, and that alone created talk, of course. What was she doing here? And she was seen *running* down the beach with Horace. Running! Well, folks thought she'd gone mad. Neither one of them should have been on the beach with the surf like that. Anyhow, as I say, that's the last anyone saw of her and it's our opin- ion that she drowned going after that little dog. You know I always think small dogs are a mistake. So easily mislaid and I have it on good authority that Horace couldn't swim."

"No, I know," says my mother, looking appalled and shocked.

"My mother saved him from drowning once," I say.

"You don't say, dear? Well, it appears Mrs. Spin- naker was not so lucky herself. And terrible for the sister because you know she'll never know for sure. Of course, none of us but you knew her well. She kept to herself, that one."

"Yes, I can't say we knew her well. We knew Horace rather better," says my mother. "He used to come for dinner now and again."

"Yes, well, she would have done better to have kept him fenced in. It appears such freedom was what did him in, did both of them in. Of course, there's always people who will say it was suicide."

"It would have to be a suicide pact," I say.

"How do you mean, dear?" says Mrs. Merriweather, leaning forward, always happy to speculate on the misfortunes of others.

"Because of Horace, of course," I say.

"I see! I see!" she says with increasing interest.

"Oh nonsense, she'd never allow Horace to kill himself," says my mother, and Mrs. Merriweather and I turn to her, happy to argue this point, when Maya comes up with a catalog and wants me to help her design a whole paper-doll village, so we go onto the porch and cut them out and occasionally the wind lifts one up and flies it out to sea.

"We should rescue them!" says Maya as we watch a woman in a long dress fly into the waves.

"Never mind," I say to her. "They're only having adventures." And then I think of Mrs. Spinnaker blown out to sea and the possible adventures she may be having but it gives me goose bumps. Mrs. Spinnaker just doesn't seem to me like the type of person to disappear at sea. She was so pragmatic. You can't see her coming to such a romantic and untidy end. I think things sometimes don't turn out the way you think. We construct these little ideas of how things are but they're like stage sets, they don't really mean anything at all. There are plans in motion that have nothing to do with your tidy little ideas. I'm sure Dorothy never expected to end up in a home in Ely all by herself and yet she will in two years when the money runs out. I think she thought she would die in the saddle.

I hear Ned being greeted by Mrs. Merriweather and his cries of astonishment as my mother tells him about Mrs. Spinnaker, and then Mrs. Merriweather, with great delight, relating all the gossip about everyone all over again.

············

We are happily settled into our lives, although not entirely, since there is still this awkwardness between me and Ned. Fortunately he is gone a lot, looking for work. Then one morning his phone rings. It is odd. We have given the number to no one in town.

Ned answers it and keeps saying "WHAT? HE *WHAT*!!!" When he hangs up he says, "Well, I'll be blamed! I'll be doggoned. I don't believe it."

"What?" says my mother. *"What?"*

"Ben has flown the coop. That was Candace. Mother called her to say that Ben went into town to deliver the three horses he sold and never came back. And apparently before he left, he turned Satan loose. Mom saw Satan from the bedroom window running across the grasslands by the pond. Candace says she kept asking Mom how she knew Ben wasn't coming back and Mom wouldn't tell her, just said that she knew and now she would have to move into the home in Ely. She was having a terrible time. She fell twice on the way to the bathroom and it took hours to get to her feet."

"Oh no," says my mother.

"And Satan's running loose on the ranch. Candace can't leave what she's doing. Everyone is back at work but me. I'll have to go. I'll have to go, Felicity. What a mess."

"What could have possessed Ben? He seemed such a nice boy."

"Nice boy, schmice boy, a nice boy would have taught Jane to ride," says Ned.

"Can we please not bring that up again?" I shout from the porch, where I have been listening in.

"I'm just saying!" Ned shouts back.

"Well, when are you going?" asks my mother.

"Tomorrow, I guess. We can't leave her like that. The airfare is going to be horrendous but we'll just have to take it out of John's bag of money."

Maya goes dashing into the kitchen from the porch. "I want to go too," she says. "I want to see Dorothy. I want to take an airplane ride."

"No, Maya, Ned's going to have his hands full," says my mother.

"Oh, let her go, Felicity," says Ned. "It will cheer

Dorothy up no end. Much more than seeing me again."

"But, Maya, you wanted to come home so badly," says my mother.

"We're going to rescue Dorothy!" says Maya.

"Maya, she's not a paper doll," I say, coming into the kitchen.

"All right, Maya," says my mother.

I cannot believe it; my mother is letting Ned take Maya. Ned is not exactly reliable. Suppose she has nightmares or sees wolf shadows on walls? Or she has hysterics because they aren't really rescuing Dorothy, they're just moving her? Or she ends up terrified on the plane? Or she finds someplace even better to hide than the hayloft?

"Let me go too," I say to my mother.

"You?" says my mother in surprise, but then it makes her happy. She is surprised I am willing to be around Ned. She sees this as a way to heal the breach, I can tell. She might have had second thoughts about letting Maya go—she knows what Maya is like too—but if I go with them, she whole-heartedly approves the plan. This will bring peace to her little family. I realize offering to go was a big mistake.

"All right, that's a very good idea, Jane. You and Maya can help Ned and cheer up Dorothy. I'm sure she'll be sad that Ben has left her in this way."

"Great. Then it's me and my girls," says Ned happily.

Northward to the Moon

The plane ride, the first for me and Maya, is so wonderful that it almost makes me cease regretting saying I would come. I insist on the window seat so that I won't have to spend the whole flight next to Ned. Also because I think putting Maya next to the window, where she can watch the ground disappear, is a mistake, but it turns out I am wrong, as she spends the whole time leaning over me trying to peer down at the ground anyway. You can just never tell with Maya.

When we get to Dorothy's house it is too late to try to do anything about Satan. Dorothy doesn't seem too badly off, just a little subdued. The kitchen is a mess. She has found handling her walker and cooking difficult and has just been opening cans and leaving dishes about. But she is clearly very pleased with herself.

"You see, Neddie," she says, "I think when the hip fully heals I can move into some kind of small apartment back in Elko. Of course, one of you will have to come and help me do the move but after that I should be fine. I just need to get the hang of things, working around the walker. But heck, once I'm healed I may not need a walker. At my age healing takes some time but I think I'm going to get around again eventually."

Ned doesn't turn from the stove, where he is making us eggs. "We'll talk about it then," he says.

Later, when he comes up to say good night—Maya and I are sleeping in Dorothy's big bed and Dorothy is sleeping downstairs—Maya says, "Can I come back when it's time to move Dorothy into an apartment?"

"Listen, Maya," says Ned. "Even if she can do a little cooking for herself, there's just too much she can't take care of alone. It would be one thing if one of us lived in Elko and could help her out."

"Why doesn't she come back with us, then?" asks Maya.

"She likes Nevada," says Ned.

"She could buy Mrs. Spinnaker's cottage. Then she'd be right next door to us," insists Maya.

"Maya, go to sleep," says Ned.

"Well, why can't she?" asks Maya as Ned turns off the light. This is rather high-handed of him as I am in here too but I think he hopes it will shut her up.

"Did you come along just to nag at me the whole time?" asks Ned.

"Turn the light back on," says Maya.

Ned turns it on and then closes the door and escapes before he has to listen to more. But when I go to brush my teeth I hear him having another angry conversation with Dorothy.

"Ben *took* the money? Why didn't you say this before? Why didn't you call the sheriff?"

"And say what? Tell the sheriff he stole money that we don't know the origin of and kept in a bag in the house? I'm more worried about my gun. He took the shotgun from where I keep it hidden in the china cupboard and all the shells. When I found the bag of money gone, that was the first thing I checked for."

"I *told* you we should've sold that thing. It should have been the *first* thing we sold."

"Whatever," says Dorothy, sounding exhausted. "He's not going to do anything so bad with it. He just wants a ranch. He'll probably light out for New Mexico or something and put a down payment on one."

"Jeez Louise, Mom. Someone's gotta know something. He's got family in town. He can't just disappear without a trace. We can get the money back, I'm pretty sure. I was counting on that money for the plane fares."

"You know what, Ned? I start to make plans and then I just get too tired. I don't have the energy to sustain that kind of thinking. It may be that I don't even care anymore. I don't seem to care about anything. I just wish he hadn't let Satan run wild like that. Now, *that* was irresponsible. And I'll pony up the plane fare. I've got a chunk in the bank from the sale of things and the ranch will bring in a pretty penny. Let's go to bed. Tomorrow's gonna be no fun and I'm tired."

The next day the first item of business is to catch Satan. The second is to go into town and see if Hank or Leeron can move back to the ranch. Ned doesn't want to leave the ranch empty when we go. The last item is to move Dorothy and her things over to Ely. This is the one we all dread.

Fortunately we can see Satan down by the pond, so Ned hands me the halter, Maya the lead rope, and he carries a bucket of grain. We make our way there. Grasses grow high around the pond, which is one reason the horses love it, and as we go through the long grasses, our eye on Satan, I suddenly hear Maya gasp. I turn to where she is looking. The ground up ahead is strewn with large lumps. Walking closer, we see what it is. There are seven dead wolves, including two dead cubs. All of them sprawled in various stages of decay.

None of us know what to say. The bodies of the dead cubs lie soft beside their mother, her body curling toward them as if even now trying to reach them. Ned moves in for a closer look but it is apparent to all of us what happened.

"They've been shot," he says. "Someone shot them."

"Dorothy's gun," I say.

"Ben," says Ned.

A sound comes from Maya and now we turn to her. There are tears running down her face. "How could he do this?" she says. "They're babies."

"I don't know, Maya," says Ned, sounding defeated. He is half kneeling, examining the carcasses, as if there is anything he can do. "I don't know why people do anything."

"Because he's a big creepy baby-hater," says Maya.

"I doubt it, Maya," says Ned sadly.

"Then why did he shoot them?" persists Maya.

"I guess we're never going to know. But he probably had reasons that made sense to him even if they don't make sense to us."

"What reasons?" demands Maya.

"I don't know, Maya," Ned says tiredly. "I don't know why John left a bag of money in the forests of British Columbia. I don't know why my father just up and left our family one day. I don't know why my mother decided to hightail it up to Fort McMurray. I don't know why Ben stole the money and stranded Dorothy. I'm telling you, I don't know why anyone does anything. People do strange things."

Ned gets up and goes toward Satan, leaving me with Maya, who has moved over to a dead baby wolf and keeps petting it.

"It's a little baby," she says.

"Remember how you were afraid of the wolves? You thought they were coming for you? They didn't even know you were there. They were just coming for water, Maya."

Satan has his nose in the grain bucket that Ned is holding so I pull Maya back to her feet and go over to help him. Satan lets himself be led back to the barn.

No one tells Dorothy about the wolves. Ned goes into town and after lunch comes back to report that Hank still has no steady job and is happy to be hired to come house-sit until the ranch sells.

We drive Dorothy over to Ely. She talks animatedly to Maya, who looks pale and quiet again.

When we get to the home we *all* turn pale and quiet. We take Dorothy in where a lot of way-too-cheerful people welcome her. It is not a terrible place but none of us would want to live here. There are very old people in wheelchairs. There is an unpleasant smell and it is too quiet. It is the type of place where despite the number of people about, you could sit and listen to the clock tick all day.

Dorothy smiles a lot but her smiles merely serve to crack the nervous tension in her face. Finally, it is time to go. Everyone hugs her. Maya cries again but by the time we get back to the ranch she has stopped. We eat a silent dinner. We are thinking of Dorothy all alone in that room.

I push some mac and cheese around on my plate.

"We'll have to make sure Hank sells the rest of the kitchen things," says Ned.

We hear the ticking of the kitchen clock.

"And the clock," says Ned. It's supposed to be funny but nobody laughs.

Maya drinks her milk slowly. Her eyes are large above the glass. It looks like she isn't drinking now, she is just tipping the glass over her mouth, giving herself a milk mustache. For some reason this irritates me. I throw my napkin on the table. It wakes up Ned, who has been lost in thought.

"Oh sweet Jesus," says Ned. "Let's go back and get her. I wouldn't leave a cat at that place."

"I thought you liked cats," says Maya as we drive back to Ely.

"It's just an expression, Maya," says Ned.

It is nine o'clock when we pull into the parking lot. We are past visiting hours and the young woman at the desk is not happy to see us. She buzzes us in but when we tell her we have changed our minds about Dorothy staying there, she sounds unsure. She doesn't know what to do.

"You don't have to do anything," says Ned. "That's the beauty of the plan." He charges up to Dorothy's room and tells her to get out of bed. He tells me and Maya to repack her things.

"I don't know if I'm allowed to just leave like this," Dorothy says, watching from her wheelchair as we buzz around the room repacking.

"It's not prison, Mom," says Ned.

"No, I know, but we'll lose the deposit and where

am I going to go now? Have you given it any thought?"

"You're going to live with us," says Maya confidently.

"All the way in Massachusetts?" asks Dorothy.

"Can we talk about this in the car, Mom?" asks Ned. "I just want to get out of here. It smells."

Dorothy doesn't say anything else but she looks baffled.

"Well, goodbye," says Dorothy to the woman as Ned wheels her past the desk.

"You'll have to leave the wheelchair with me," says the woman. "You can't take it outside. That's our wheelchair."

We help Dorothy to her walker and she hobbles to the car. As soon as we all get into it, Maya says, "There. That's better."

For some reason this makes us all laugh.

After we drive for a bit, Ned tells Dorothy about Mrs. Spinnaker's cottage.

"I don't know," says Dorothy. "It sounds kind of wet to me. Living by the ocean. I like a dry climate myself."

"Look at the moon," says Maya, bouncing in her

seat. She is very happy. She is sitting in the back with Dorothy so I am up front with Ned. "Moon milk."

"We saw a full moon like that in B.C.," I explain to Dorothy, turning around. "Hanging at the edge of the highway. My mother said it looked like you could drive to it."

"I know exactly what you're talking about. I've seen that too! A moon you could drive to. Hanging right at the edge of the highway," says Dorothy. "I had all the kids in the car and we were headed north away from Edmonton and I didn't know where we were going, I just knew we weren't going back *there*, and I thought, That's where we'll go. I can drive all the way to the moon. We'll just keep going northward to the moon."

Then she and Maya fall asleep in the back. We hear their soft snores.

"Maybe she was on her way to the moon but she only made it as far as Fort McMurray," I whisper to Ned. "Maybe she ran out of gas."

He startles. I haven't initiated conversation with him for some time now. Then he sits and stares ahead down the highway, considering. Finally he turns his head slightly and says, "I don't know but I don't expect it matters, Bibles, whether I understand why she did it or not. It's what happened."

"Strange and inconvenient things," I say. I put my feet up on the dashboard and scrounge around in my pocket until I find my gum. "Want a piece?" He shakes his head.

We go back to peering out through the big front windshield. But companionably. The desert sky is full of stars.

Epilogue

I sit next to Ned on the plane. We are seated two and two across the aisle because both Maya and I want window seats, although Maya spends most of her time playing cards with Dorothy, who has a seemingly endless tolerance for Go Fish. Ned and I read. He has called my mom and warned her that Dorothy is coming with us. Ned says my mother sounds delighted.

"Well, she would be," he says, shaking his head. "She never fails to astonish and fascinate me, your mother."

When we get home there are more practical arrangements. My mother has bought an inflatable bed for her and Ned, which she sets up in the living room, giving Dorothy their bedroom. Getting Dorothy in over the sand is a bit of a trick. She has to be carried everywhere, even out to the picnic table when we eat, so it's a good thing she is so slight.

As we put bowls on the picnic table, my mother gasps.

"For a second I thought I saw Mrs. Spinnaker," she explains. "It must be her sister, they look so alike. Why don't I go over and ask her to have dessert with us and we'll find out what she's asking for Mrs. Spinnaker's cottage?"

"It looks like a wet place to live," says Dorothy uncertainly. "And all this sand."

"But you'd be next door to us," says Maya.

"Well, yes, that would make it all worthwhile, wouldn't it, dear?" says Dorothy, putting her hand on top of Maya's.

My mother and I go next door to see Mrs. Spinnaker's sister. "Why do you think Dorothy and Maya like each other so much?" I ask my mother.

"I don't know, but you see, there are always upsides in these situations," she says. I didn't know she regarded Dorothy as a situation. She may have given herself away a little there but I don't pursue it.

My mother knocks on the door and when it opens we are flabbergasted. There indeed is Mrs. Spinnaker's sister, but also Mrs. Spinnaker. In the back we hear Horace barking.

"Forevermore!" says my mother.

"Yes, my reaction exactly," says Mrs. Spinnaker's sister.

"Mrs. Spinnaker, you've returned!"

"Obviously," says Mrs. Spinnaker. "As have you."

"Yes, yes, I hadn't thought of it that way," says my mother.

"So there you are," says Mrs. Spinnaker.

My mother does not know what to say. She can hardly say what she came to say, which is, We want to buy your house. Finally she just asks them both over for dessert.

"And Horace too, of course," she says.

I don't think Mrs. Spinnaker would have come but her sister has already accepted enthusiastically so she has to follow suit. She gets Horace and we troop back over.

When Ned, who has been clearing the table,

sees her he says, "OH NO! Mrs. Spinnaker! You've come back!"

I know he is thinking that the plan to put his mother in Mrs. Spinnaker's house is foiled now but it certainly doesn't sound right. He quickly explains himself but Mrs. Spinnaker is still left with the impression that Ned is either (a) an idiot or (b) the type of person who says Oh no when he sees you coming. Either way it puts her in a tetchy frame of mind.

We have dessert, and afterward as we sit, gently leaning our full stomachs forward toward the table like you do after a too-abundant meal, my mother finally says, "So, Mrs. Spinnaker, where were you?"

"Hawaii," says Mrs. Spinnaker.

"Vacation?" asks my mother.

"None of your business," says Mrs. Spinnaker.

"She was having a love affair," whispers her sister. I don't know why she whispers it. It is designed for all to hear. But we can't react. Obviously Mrs. Spinnaker doesn't want to talk about it.

"Well, I'm glad to see Horace is all right," says my mother.

"Why wouldn't he be?" asks Mrs. Spinnaker grumpily.

"There are some folks who thought he drowned," says my mother falteringly.

"There's always some folks thinking some things," says Mrs. Spinnaker, and this, I think, pretty much says it all.

After that, we go to bed. The surf is wild and we hear the waves splashing soothingly. It is, I realize, like my own deepest breathing. That's why the surf is so soothing. It is as if it breathes for me so I can take a break. Sometimes I think I am almost frantic, trying to keep myself safe, to keep everyone I love safe. Wanting things to be all right and people to be happy. I think everyone is like this but the sound of the ocean makes me think I can relax my vigilance. Something will breathe for me while I sleep. Something will breathe for Maya. Maybe our heroic measures aren't really needed. But what if they are? I don't have to know tonight, I think, and fall asleep to the crash and scraping of tiny pebbles being pulled out to sea along the ancient shore.

In the morning Ned and my mother and Dorothy are talking around the kitchen table. There are a coffeepot and a plate of muffins on the table and they look like they are digging in for a long complicated discussion. Then I see why.

"Now what?" says Dorothy. "I thought the point of moving here was to live next door to you."

"It was going to be a great setup," says Ned, shaking his head. "This just bungs up everything. I suppose you could move in here. I know Felicity doesn't mind."

"It's still pretty wet," says Dorothy. "And there isn't a lot of space."

"We could build an addition," says my mother uncertainly.

"I suppose it would cost less than buying Mrs. Spinnaker's place," says Dorothy with equal uncertainty.

The table gets pretty quiet after that.

············

It was one thing when Dorothy was temporary but now that she's someone who will be here permanently, it is different. Our house seems vastly more crowded and someone is always in the living area.

I don't think the boys mind but even Maya seems to find it cramped. And Dorothy isn't just a stage prop. The willing victim of our kindness. She is used to her own house. She has opinions about everything and especially about Ned.

Ned has his own opinions and one is that she should stop calling him Neddie. "It drives me crazy," he mutters to no one in particular. "It's like fingernails on a chalkboard."

Then one day Ned comes home from pounding the pavement and brings cupcakes and steaks and potato chips.

"You got a job!" says my mother.

"YES!" He grabs her and twirls her in a circle.

"I wouldn't do that if I were you, Ned," says Dorothy from her perch on the porch. "You could throw your back out."

"What kind of a job?" I ask.

"Teaching Japanese!" he says exultantly. "Night school! And there's some translation work for me too!"

"You don't speak Japanese," says Dorothy.

"Yes he does, it's *French* he doesn't speak," corrects Maya.

We are all happy and Ned is making a fire on the beach to grill the steaks but Dorothy is uncomfortable. It is too damp and chilly, she says. It makes her hip hurt. The sand gets into her food and why can't we eat inside, why are we always eating outside like animals?

By the end of the week Ned has found a nice convalescent hospital in Lincoln that can take Dorothy until her hip is totally healed and he finds a room for her in Mrs. Bedlington's boardinghouse in town. He assures her both places are very dry. Also it is just two doors down from Nellie's church, where we used to go every Sunday. Even Maya can walk there alone.

Ned moves Dorothy into the convalescent hospital and suddenly our house feels enormous to me. We have a steak dinner that night although no one says that it is to celebrate.

"I don't care," Ned has taken to saying enigmatically and out of context. "I'm no saint."

Ginny comes home from camp finally and we take many sunrise walks on the beach to catch up. We go at sunrise because I love the fresh clean morning beach before anyone else gets to it and

Ginny says she can't sleep late after a summer at camp. "They made us get up at the crack of dawn!" she complains. "It's horrible what some people put you through in the name of fun."

I tell her everything that has happened this year, some of which she has heard before in letters, but the Nevada part is all new. Mostly she seems interested in Ben. She agrees that what Ned did was terrible.

"Oh my God, I would have simply died. I would have died!" she says.

"Exactly!" I say with satisfaction. "Although it did turn out he was of a criminally bent nature."

"Never mind that," says Ginny. "Tell me again what he looked like."

I have already told Ginny this a dozen times, and also how he would vault right over the fence into the ring. She finds it fascinating. "I would have thought you would go for a more cerebral type. But I applaud your taste," she says. "Tell me again about his shoulders."

"Sometimes you really are shallow," I say affectionately.

"Well, of course I am, darling, I'm in fashion,"

says Ginny. This business of calling me darling is a new affectation that needs immediate squelching. She has sorely missed my influence in the year we've been apart.

"OH!" I say. "I can't believe I forgot to tell you this—guess who is Maya's father?"

"Who? Who? Mr. Fordyce!" says Ginny.

"NO! Worse! H.K.," I say.

"How do you know? Did your mother tell you?"

"Not in so many words but she said that she was worried about insanity in Maya's family history! That made it obvious. Crazy Caroline!"

"You know Crazy Caroline is out again?"

"Never mind that. Think! That also means he probably isn't *my* father."

"True, true," says Ginny, but I can tell her mind is elsewhere. We walk a bit in silence and then she says, "Is that all your mother said, that there was mental illness in Maya's family history?"

I think back. "Yes."

"And from this you deduce that it must be H.K.?"

"You're saying it's not?"

"Well . . . think about it, Jane. The clothes hanger

man wasn't exactly the poster boy for normalcy. I mean, what do you call someone roaming all over the country with only the clothes on his back?"

"Oh," I say. "I hadn't thought of that."

"And Mr. Fordyce lives in a trailer and reads books all day. Okay, that's not so strange, but who knows what lurks in his family? You don't know him well enough to say. We should go and ask a few questions, you know, in a roundabout way that won't raise his suspicions. And then there's Ned."

"Ned?"

"Well, from the way you describe them, his whole family sounds crazy to me. I mean, the mother moves them all up to some remote outpost for no reason and his sister sees the Virgin Mary in her food."

"Oh," I say. "And I suppose spending the year pretending you can teach French is pretty loopy."

"I kind of like that about him. There's something so, sort of, free about Ned . . . ," says Ginny. "I mean, my mom and dad had normal upbringings and they never got schlepped up to Fort McMurray one night and they would never think of pretending to teach French."

"Yeah," I say, but now I am deflated. "I thought I had it all figured out."

"People are nuts," Ginny concludes, then she does a little twirl. "What do you think of this dress? I made it myself this spring."

Ginny wants to be a dress designer. It is not her dress twirling in the wind that I see, though, it is the sun beginning its arduous luminous climb through the sky. A pair of gulls flies by, tilted sideways in the wind, cackling messages we cannot understand. But they can't understand us either. It doesn't mean, I think, that none of us are making sense.

"Come on, " I say. "Let's go to my house for breakfast. I'm starving."

Maya and her new friend, Rachel, are sitting on the beach playing paper dolls when we get there.

"My mom and Maya ran into Rachel and her mother in the convalescent hospital visiting Dorothy," I explain to Ginny. "Rachel's grandmother is in there too. Rachel and Maya used to play in the block corner together in kindergarten and when they saw each other Maya asked her for a sleepover."

"Good for Maya," says Ginny.

I nod. Maya looks happy and absolutely fine, just like my mother predicted.

We head toward the porch. Ned is sitting on the steps.

"Hi, Ned," says Ginny. "So my mom says Mrs. Bedlington says your mom is moving in there in a month."

"I'm no saint," says Ned, wearing the haunted hangdog expression he has had since his mother moved to town.

"Jeez, what's with him?" whispers Ginny.

"Oh, he's just not forgiving himself or anyone else since another highfalutin' idea he had about how things ought to be never panned out," I say.

"I thought his mother didn't want to live here," says Ginny.

"She didn't! He didn't want it either. I don't think anyone did. But don't worry, my mom is jollying him out of it," I say as my mother comes out on the porch and hands Ned a plate.

"Oh, but, Ned, you must be a saint. Because, look! The Virgin Mary is appearing on your toast!" says my mother, and laughs uproariously.

"She's spent the last twenty-four hours putting the Virgin Mary on all his food," I say to Ginny.

"Your mother is jollying him along by putting sacred apparitions in his food?" says Ginny.

"Yes," I say.

"Let's go make toast," says Ginny. "Without religious miracles. Just toast."

"I think that can be arranged," I say as Ginny heads into the kitchen.

I stay and watch the waves for a minute. Then I go inside, leaving my mother and Ned sitting on the porch steps, an arm around each other, watching Maya play.

The next day Ned is gone.

He left a note.

about the author

Polly Horvath is the highly acclaimed author, most recently, of *My One Hundred Adventures*, which *School Library Journal*, in a starred review, called "Horvath's most luminescent, beautifully written novel yet" and *Kirkus Reviews*, also in a starred review, described as "witty, wise and wonderful." Her other books include *The Canning Season*, winner of the National Book Award and the CLA's Young Adult Book Award; *Everything on a Waffle*, a Newbery Honor Book, an ALA Notable Book and winner of the Mr. Christie's Book Award and the Sheila A. Egoff Children's Literature Prize; *The Corps of the Bare-boned Plane*, winner of the Sheila A. Egoff Children's Literature Prize; and *The Vacation*, winner of the *Child Magazine* Best Book Award and the Chocolate Lily Award. Polly Horvath lives in Metchosin, British Columbia.